EnDearing Minds

First published 2014

EnDearing Minds
Annual student anthology 2014
The University of Nottingham
School of Education

UNITED KINGDOM · CHINA · MALAYSIA

BA (Hons) Creative and Professional Writing
BA (Hons) Fine Art

Acknowledgements

Running the anthology this year was an amazing experience. We met so many talented individuals and got to read fantastic work. Seeing this project from start to finish has taught us so much about the publishing process, creativity and people.

This project has definitely had its share of difficulties. We wanted to bring the work into the digital age to compete against the growing eBook market which created its own set of challenges. However, thanks to all of the people we worked with, we succeeded.

We owe a special thanks to Nicola Valentine, Heidi Mather, Julie Garlick, Nick Mobbs and Pippa Hennessey for their guidance and expertise. Without their support the project would not have gotten off the ground.

Our editorial team deserves the highest praise. They helped us shape and mould the book into what it is now. Thank you to Sara Assumani, Andrea Bowd, Elizabeth Cooper, Giulia Donati, Tom Farrell, Oliver Gillespie, Elisa Gradwohl, Eleanor Hemsley, Andrew Henley, Elizabeth Jamieson, Kimberly Jamison, Amy Maidment, Liam Powell, Cheryll Rawling, Tim Shelley and Bethany Sirl, who were led by Head Editors Oliver Gillespie and Liam Powell.

We also thank Bethany Sirl for helping us to launch ourselves into the eBook market by helping creating our eBook as well as proofreading our book.

Finally, we have to thank all of our contributors. Without their brilliant and diverse work, this anthology would not exist.

Eleanor Hemsley and Kimberly Jamison

Contents

Never-Ending
By Sara Assumani

A pink hue settles on the mountains
and my mind starts to ponder when my internal doors will open again.
When will I fall back down the hole or walk through the wardrobe to the untainted world of mystery and wonder?
My mind is chained by my mind.
And though my feet can take me further than the edges of the world, over into infinity,
I will find nothing but a blank sheet of consciousness waiting to swallow me.
Take me back to the fleeting moment when my mind was a door and I was the key. I unlocked and found the eighth wonder of the world to have it slither away back into yesterday. And the day before, and the day before that.
Where am I now? Where is it now? Am I still me?
A pink hue settles on the mountains and I begin to ponder, what life used to mean from the other side of my mental block.

In Character
By Alexandra Adamson

There is a place
always kept empty
the place where
a heart should be.

It's not that
it's misplaced
more rather,
an absence of it.

A space always
empty
waiting to be completed
with a part that will never be
or ever existed.

Shadows and Tall Trees
By Andrew Henley

Paige Anderson stood in the spiky shadow of the tree that had loomed over her all her life. Its coarse skin was tattooed with lover's initials and its branches reached up to the summer sky, grasping it tightly, pulling it over Paige like a security blanket. Paige's skin was as contoured as the tree itself, light creases forming in her loose, pale skin, emanating out from the corners of her lips, nose, eye sockets, throat and fingers.

30 years ago today, Paige's body was young and pure and curvy; her hips wrapped in dark, highwaist denim shorts, leaving her legs bare. Her hair was coiffed and black like a mudflap pinup. Jason's car was rusty and humid, the interior tinged with the smell of escapism doused in smoke and alcohol.

Jason wound his window up. He leant across Paige, brushing his ear to her breasts and her heartbeat, feeling them both rise. He removed a tightly wrapped joint from his pocket and held it between his teeth as he drove. He took his hands off the wheel, using one to hold the old brass lighter to thumb the flame into existence, while the other rose out of habit to shield the fresh flame from an imagined wind. He took a deep drag. As he opened his mouth, a thick, hallucinogenic fog poured out like hot soup.

He handed it to Paige.

"It's called hotboxing."

That was all he said for the rest of the drive.

Paige pushed the joint into her pink painted preacher's daughter lips and took an intoxicating inhale. She tensed her barely teenaged body with all her will to not splutter.

Looking through her dark sunglasses, Paige saw melting world disappear and blur. She blew on the clear glass and wrote her name on the temporary notepaper of condensation. She could feel Jason's rough and calloused hand swimming in the unexplored lake of her thigh.

They arrived at the forest's edge. Tall trees behind young, sprouting bushes. Jason stopped on the loosely packed clay of the dirt track. Paige climbed out of the car and slid her hands into the back pockets of her shorts, her sleeveless, white, polka-dot vest wispy in the rhythm of the wind. Her loveheart tattoo was new and crimson; 30 years later, time has stolen her deep red rebellion.

Jason's car came off the line a proud navy blue, before rust had gnawed through the chassis. It rattled as he climbed out and locked the door with a heavy clunk. He put his arm around Paige, pulling her close to him like a strong legged spider. Jason was 25, a day labourer who had twice served time for assault. His skin was firm, his body cornet shaped, with muscles sculpted by prison sentences and shovels. Paige wanted to see Jason naked. She had no idea what was between his legs. Men on T.V. and in magazines or movies always covered up. Apparently some girls at school had seen dirty movies where they didn't, but Paige thought that was a load of crap. She wasn't particularly interested in that, anyway. It was idle curiosity. She wanted to lace her fingers through his chest hair, grabbing his firm buttocks and scratching his strong legs. He had a tear drop tattoo that he told Paige represented a murder he had gotten away with. Paige had chosen him to anger her father; it was Jason or a Jew.

As they walked through the forest, thin blades of long grass grazed Paige's leg, tickling her into giggles. Their path was not clearly marked, and they often had to wade through soft, swampy earth, muddying their soles. There was a dense canopy that blackened their world; at times the only light was thin, piercing swords that fought its way through narrow holes in the leaves.

"It'll be worth it when we get there," Jason said as he dragged her by the hand through the weeds.

Paige's mouth felt dry after her first smoke, and her mind reeled in the uncharted territory of losing her drug virginity. Creatures and eyes seemed to emerge from the dense foliage, laughing at her, grinning with huge teeth and watching her every move.

Eventually they came to a small, secluded hill with a single tree at its peak. The tree had no marks then. It was smoother; perhaps it was happier. Jason pulled a switchblade knife out of his front pocket and slammed it deep into the untouched bark. Paige pulled it out and fondled the cool handle as if she were an expert.

"You know what we should do?" Paige asked, flicking the switchblade in and out of its stowaway compartment. "We should carve our initials into the tree."

"Whatever," Jason said.

He took a long drag on a new joint and admired the sprayed out sunlight on the horizon.

Paige carved 'P.A. + J.' into the tree.

"What's your surname?"

"Lebowitz."

Paige added the 'L' to the tree and thought, "Cool. He's a Jew as well."

Drawing the horizontal line of the 'L', Paige felt Jason push his body up against her back. The joint was still in his mouth; the burnt, peppery tip was blisteringly close to Paige's nostril.

Through gritted teeth acting as a vice on his joint, Jason said, "Now we'll have something to remember this by."

His hands slithered under her vest, his palms scratching lightly as they cupped her small, blossoming breasts.

"No, Jason," Paige said.

She tried to push him away but he was an immovable pillar. There was no escape to the front either; caught between a tree and a hard place.

"Don't be like that," Jason said.

His joint dropped to the grass below them, smouldering until Jason's foot ground the embers away.

"No!"

Paige tried to sound stern but it came out quivering and desperate.

Jason's hands reached around to her front and forced open the zip of her shorts with a metallic pop.

Paige spun quickly, tearing Jason's hand open on the jagged edge of her zip. Instinctively, Paige stabbed Jason in the chest with his own switchblade. There was a crack of cartilage and a narrow jetstream of red as the knife pierced Jason between two ribs. Paige let go and it remained imbedded, the glossy wooden handle reaching out like a small, ineffective limb. He fell back against the soft earth and gasped for air wordlessly. The dense muscles in his neck strained and bulged as he fought against the contractions of his narrowing throat. Paige put her hands on his chest, compressing the wound, feeling blood and life leak out of him with every slowing thump of his threading pulse. Flecks of blood spat up and disappeared in the polka-dots of her top.

Her hands were stained with a deep, oxygenated, red syrup. Her fresh, smooth skin looked like it was acne cursed, and sticky clots of flesh were tangled in her blonde hair like bubblegum. She took Jason's keys and ran back through the forest, past the watching, laughing eyes. She opened up the boot of his car, grabbed his shovel and returned to the dead man on the hill.

The wood of the shovel handle drank up the wet blood from her palms. Paige dug a deep hole and buried Jason in it, then covered it over and packed the dirt tight. The crushed remnants of his joint marked his headstone.

There Paige stood, 30 years later. The tree was taller, and stained with the presence of other lovers. It had been living off Jason's decaying nutrients for the last half a century. No one had come looking for Jason. He was a drifter, a day labourer. No family.

On her way to the tree, Paige passed by Jason's car. Rain and rust had stolen chunks from the front and rear bumpers; they looked like sharp jaws, taking bites out of stray cars that passed by on the solitary dirt track. A predator, a haunting phantom for lonely drivers.

Paige ran her wrinkled fingers across the tree's bark. Her fingertips felt the knifed imprints of letters left by other lovers.

"30 years is long enough," Paige said.

She swung her axe into the spine of the tree, wheezing under the effort. The handle of the axe was smooth and porous, wicking the sweat off her palms. The paper embers of the joint that had blown away decades ago were not Jason's headstone, Paige realized. The tree was. And it had been desecrated repeatedly by other peoples' happiness. With every chop, Paige cut half an inch deeper into the tree's core. She let the heavy, dull blade rest against the earth as she regained the strength for another tired chop. Eventually, the tree collapsed, its branches still outstretched towards the sky.

Evergreen Roof
By Kaya Gromocki

Taken in Alderly Edge, Cheshire

Insomnia
By Sean Keenan

Stay in bed and try to sleep.
Insomnia takes control and it's back up on your feet,
Hobble down rickety stairs, to locate the creative domain,
Clock ticking abrasively, as you look for inspiration yet again.

The blank screen looms, the cursor taunts,
Rubbing coarse fingers across wrinkled brow you wait.
Think of something, anything to remove this vacant state,
Type the first words, the embers begin to rekindle a flame.

Finally you're in it and try to write as much as you can
Because this moment, you may never get again,
Scratching the barrel of your mind, ignore the mistakes
If you stop typing to correct them, it could be too late.

But what inspires the writing, the linking of the lines?
It's the bitter taste you have when wasting time,
The unification of those that can relate
And the scathing reality that the words may only meet your tastes.

It may be hard but persevere and keep writing,
Every moment could create something great
Embrace the time when thoughts are found,
Know to surrender when the moment is gone.

Running, after three years

By Adrian Buckner

I am your stitch. I come one mile in.
Drag me home another half mile.

Drag me through the last three years,
through that venomous promotion,

the corridors of dull enmity,
their midnight blinking screens.

Drag me through the cluttered outhouse
and the shut door dumping room,

past brave words misremembered
and a promise now reframed.

Drag me through new sympathies
of back pain and sleeplessness.

Drag me toward that distant train
across the breaking dawn,

I'll drive from you a stride for home
where you'll sink

to the grasp above your knees
and heave the whole of it.

Kill Them with Kindness
By Leigh Campbell

Kill them with kindness, her grandmother had always said. Natasha hadn't always agreed. For a while, she had tried with fierce determination to live by her grandmother's words, but there was only so much taunting, so much hair pulling and cutting comments a young girl of six could take, especially an orphaned one. As Natasha grew older she learned that she could not kill people with kindness, but knives, well, knives worked a treat.

But knives were messy and personal; two things that Natasha was not. Nevertheless, she had been so young, only twelve, when she was sent on her first assignment that she had found comfort in the steel glint of blades cutting deep into taut flesh. She had revelled in the sense of power and control it instilled within her. She barely questioned the orders from above to kill – she was just doing her job, she didn't care much was it was.

By the age of 16, she had convinced herself that anyone who was not working with her was working against her, and that they were the ones who had killed her family. Every night she saw the house engulfed by flames and every morning she saw the ashes scattered by the wind. The recesses of her mind were the darkest dungeons, ones that she knew she shouldn't enter but couldn't seem to stop herself from doing so.

Her eyes glinted as she handled weaponry that she shouldn't have even known existed – bullets that shot from bracelets, electric currents that sprang from disguised lipstick cases to incapacitate even the strongest men – and malice ran through her blood as she plunged the blades into the hearts of those she had been told had destroyed her. Sometimes she made it quick and easy – jump in, kill the target, jump out – but sometimes she made it a game. How long could they last before they screamed? Before they cried out for mercy? How long could she take it before she felt her stomach turn? How long could she fight in critical combat before she got bored of pretending she might lose?

No, knives were not kind, not to their victims and not to their owners. Natasha soon discovered that the stains she wiped from her blade would not wipe as easily from her mind, no matter how hard she scrubbed. She began to dwell, the contorted faces of those she had so ruthlessly slaughtered converging on her night after night. She stopped sleeping.

At 19, she was so far in that she could not even begin to imagine where the exit might be. When she tried to get out, create a new life for herself in some remote place, they found her and tried to kill her. Her life or her service, that is what they had said. She was their prized assassin, their bullet straight through the heart. With the realization that she was condemned to this life forever came the realization that guns were much kinder than knives. Guns meant shooting from a distance and not seeing the light leave the eyes of her victim, a view that used to make her smile. Guns meant that if she concentrated hard enough, she might not even hear their screams.

The discovery that it was not her enemies but her allies who had killed her family allowed Natasha to break free of her chains and kill them in the kindest way possible. She did not turn around, did not flinch, as the bomb exploded, wrenching apart the very foundations of the prison she had called a home and tearing, limb from limb, the jailers she had called her family.

Ephemeral Galaxy
By Uta Feinstein

Debris

By Eleanor Hemsley

The explosion echoes through the night, the heat from it singeing the small hairs at the back of my neck. Fiery wood and brick fall around me, their flames slowly diminishing in the rain. I continue to walk.

I take a cigarette out of my pocket, bend over, and light it on a piece of burning debris at my feet. I lift it to my smiling lips and inhale. The taste is somewhat sweeter tonight.

Prom.
By Kaya Gromocki

A hall heaving with seven years of supressed opinions,
I am a spinning girl, flitting through the crowd,
Running from him again.
I stand in my cascading red prom dress, lost and swathed in a magenta shroud.
We eat our way through three courses as I drown in the rosè,
I dance through the Queens Hotel, running from him again.

A lost girl, flooded in crimson.

Cinderella shoes clatter on the spiral steps,
Glitter hails down on the concrete with each footfall,
But you are a leech, cuckoo nested in the coat of a lost kitten
And tonight, you shed your selkie skin.
'Leave the twirling girl' you say, 'leave her to act as Ophelia'
She's just running from him again.

Silver tears swim with the flaring ribbons, flamenco red.

The climax has come and you lean back to see if I'll implode or explode,
Intoxicated with hysteria I stumble through the chaos,
You shake your head and crown me a crowd pleaser.
You drained me dry of comfort and left me none for myself
And now you roll your eyes and watch me break at the seams.
The bar blurs as I balance three drinks, a drunken jester
Giving everyone a laugh because I'm running from him again.

No amount of glitter and gowns are going to give this night a fairy-tale ending

So we sit on the pavement outside because the wicked witch has gone
And we'll smoke our sorrows out until the sun rises over the city.
I won't run from him again.

I lie.

Brew
By Amy Maidment

Dog friendly, snob friendly,
'Please just buy our coffee' friendly;
Vinyl records, brass contraptions,
No wifi to cause distractions.
Sarcasm and coffee art,
Tiny stools and cups and lattes,
Dazed and small and cramped and cosy,
Busy, bright, and somehow homely.
Hipster sounds and hipster people,
Hipster church, and hipster steeple.
Chalkboard menus, shiny things,
Do you want a coffee maybe?

Abundance
By Uta Feinstein

Good afternoon
By Georgina Wilding

On the train to a ghost town,
visiting the other halves of me.
A cold shoulder in my stomach,
tutting tongues in my forehead.

I gaze up from my book
and look. A field of cows with
a dull stream of rain water
crashing through the middle
made me think of intrusion.

I thought it, in this case,
peaceful.
Until a magpie lands
right in my eye line.

Thinking only of the disaster
chugging towards me, I salute,
with a flap of leather and a
chime of metal bracelet.

“Good afternoon, Mr Magpie”
I beg. Good afternoon.

Them
By Charlotte Porter

She woke.

It had happened before: she had woken up in the bed that wasn't hers, wasn't the one with the scratchy linen sheets, and startled herself. It took a few moments for her to come to and acclimatize to the… well, it wasn't a room, was it? A room implies something homely, something friendly, something inviting. A room swells with warm memories. It hums with benevolence. A room smells like fresh dew on an April lawn, or Grandmother Thelma's creased palms. She tried to take in her surroundings but the candle flickered feebly, gasping for air, clinging to its last breath of life. She could see her shadow in the withering light, half a body propped up on a foldaway bed. The shadow raised a hand to its head; her hair was just as greasy as it had been the night before. Then again, it would probably stay that way until the next water ration.

She rose from the bed, wincing slightly as she felt the bones in her wrist grind against each other. It was a pain she'd have to grow accustomed to. There was no way she could afford a medic.

There was a tremor, a rumble from above. The rumble broke into a brigade of footsteps that broke into a thunderous drum. She tensed, hoping, praying that They weren't coming for her; that she hadn't been found. The stone walls that stood as her barrier to the world seemed futile, pathetic. She closed her eyes and waited, but the footsteps died down and disappeared. The ceiling quivered, and a rainfall of silver-like powder showered onto the floor. She was safe.

At the top of the stairs the door creaked open; a low groan of agony. Grey light glowed through the crack, casting a vertical strip of light onto the wall opposite her. It reminded her of a skyscraper, like the ones that used to dominate the landscape of London or narrate the city of New York. Oh, how they would tower over the horizon; majestic sculptures that silhouetted the sky; outstretched arms reaching out to Olympus; dynamic defenders, enclosing the city.

A subtle breeze roused a chorus of creaks from the door hinges. She went outside.

Light was trying to break through the layers of dust and haze that lingered in the air but an ebony darkness hung heavy overhead. There was no way of telling the time. Everyone had long since given up on that. The wind moaned through the bare branches of the trees and unsettled the soot that had blanketed the ground. Her breath came out in puffs of wispy clouds that billowed from her lips. It wasn't the cold that crept under her skin, more the total emptiness that echoed in the air.

He stood with his back to her, his shirt hanging loosely off his back so she could see the scars that crept up his shoulder. His arms were hugged around his chest, because of the chill or because everyone felt lonely nowadays, she couldn't tell.

"Liam?"

He turned, but only his head, his angular jaw now facing her way.

"I didn't mean to wake you, Freja."

His voice was low and hollow, broken by pain that was, nowadays, normal to live with. It roused a burning feeling inside her, the feeling she'd felt the night before as his fingers wound around the arch of her neck and the bulges of his spine bowed over her vulnerable figure. The scratches on her thighs stung where his loneliness had dug into her flesh.

"You didn't."

He turned away once more and his shoulders tensed, the muscles rippling in his back. He gave nothing away with his body language, other than a disturbing mysteriousness. Not that Freja knew him well. She didn't want to know anything more about him, even if he was a neighbour. He was merely a safety; protection; someone who filled a gap. She had accepted the fact that when she looked into his russet eyes there would be no emotion. No furtive desire or unspoken passion that she may have once lusted for. She would merely see a reflection of her own impassive feelings, and that was all they were to each other.

"Are we safe here?"

He nodded, "For now."

"I heard something."

Liam didn't reply. He let a silence fall between them, then added, "It's late."

"Is it?" She looked up at the sky hopelessly. "You can never tell anymore."

He pointed out to the horizon where a faint white light flickered, dimming in and out like that of a lighthouse tower.

"It's the Watch." His tone was dull, dead of expression. "That light will be on until morning."

She thought about the time when morning was associated with the warmth of a new day. Now all it was a sign that you'd made it through the night.

"Will you go home now?" He was looking at her now. She wasn't sure if this was him asking her to leave. It certainly didn't sound like an invitation to stay. In all honesty, she wasn't even sure if she wanted to – stay, that is. Her mouth was raw. Her hair was thick with the dust of the concrete ceiling that had showered down on her as the bed pounded over and over and over against the wall.

"I think so."

Now he was closer, so close that she could see his protruding collarbones, his hollow cheeks. What once might have been a romantic moment was now merely an ordinary gesture, as he stroked her face and murmured, "Be careful."

For a moment, she was reminded of someone. A man with velvety fingers that would comb through her hair as she lay with her head in his lap. A man who spoke with a tender tolerance, a warm heart. There was always devotion in his eyes, a loyalty and a bravery he proved when he locked her in the basement of their house and sacrificed himself. A determination and an honour that he conserved right till the end, as They came for him, as They took him away.

Liam had gone. She began running.

There was nothing that terrified her more than the silence. Yes, she was running so They wouldn't catch her, but she was also running to hear the blood roaring in her ears. She was running to hear her raucous pants, the soles of her feet slapping the ground. The faster she ran, the further she got away from the grave tranquillity. The gloom was a silent, ominous poison, seeping out of the drains, bleeding through the cracks in the pavement. She stopped at the road. Liam's house was just about visible across the barren landscape, through the haze. Some time ago there used to be houses in between; friendly faces. Not anymore.

She wasn't far now. She began running again, this time conscious of every shadow, every slight rustle. They came when you weren't expecting, emerging through the fog like ghosts. She reached her door, stepping over the pile of red bricks, fumbling with the keys as she hurriedly tried to get inside. They jangled together, a chilling tune ringing in the air. If she didn't hurry They might hear her… she rammed the keys into the lock and threw open the door. An icy gasp of air greeted her. She slammed the door closed and drew the bolt.

The inside of the house was barren and dark. Once upon a time she may have turned on the light, but she couldn't remember the last time she had a bulb. Instead she fumbled blindly forward. Her hands felt for the wall, guiding her along the familiar path to the hallway, then to the banister, and then to her bedroom, all the while resisting the stench of the damp and the neglect that infected the house like a plague.

She felt the iron handle of her bedroom door under her quivering hand. Relieved, she let herself in. The window was open – had she closed it before she left? She couldn't remember… she must have forgotten to. The curtains danced in the wind, dresses billowing in a breeze. Perhaps if she had a view of a river that ran alongside her house, she would have sat on the windowsill for a while. Perhaps if there was sunlight streaming across the carpet, showering the walls with brilliant shadows and chinks of honey gold, she might have left the window open. Yet the longer the curtains danced the more she could feel the presence of the poison seeping into the carpet. She closed the windows. The curtains stopped dancing.

Drained, she climbed into bed, wincing slightly as she felt the bones in her wrist grind against each other. The scratchy linen sheets welcomed her with open arms, wrapping her in a familiar embrace, hugging her close to the mattress. Her head was heavy with fatigue. She raised a hand to her head, running her fingers through her greasy hair. Usually she would have lit a candle, a gesture of warmth to raise her spirits, but tonight she lay looking up at the cracked ceiling. She thought of the smell of fresh dew on an April lawn; of Grandmother Thelma's creased palms. She thought of something homely, something friendly; something inviting. And then she wondered how much more of this darkness she could take. With a sigh of exhaustion and defeat, she closed her eyes.

Shame.

If she lit a candle she would have seen one of Them standing behind the door.

Next Door
By Uta Feinstein

Nuthall Island
By T.R.J. Shelley

Manmade, handcrafted with blood and toil
No sand, just concrete sprinkled with soil
Enclosed by an alcove of parallel trees
That in fall sees the path covered in leaves

In winter the snow lies thick, undisturbed
Until dauntless travellers wade through, undeterred
Whilst in summer birds flutter and sing
And the humming of crickets gives out a great ring

People walk at peace with their dogs
Content with contemplation and the whirring of cogs
As they struggle over great concepts such as the meaning of life
Or seek refuge in their minds sheltered from daily strife

There are no coconuts here
No seas to be seen
For the Island is a memory
And dreams of the silver screen

There Was a Little Girl, Who Had a Little Curl
By Tracey Holland
An excerpt from the memoirs, 'Born in the Change'.

When I was young, things were much simpler. Our days were filled with fun and laughter, our imaginations brimming, taking in everything around us. We took every day one at a time and had no time for tomorrow. Hey, we had lots of tomorrows, so why worry?

My weekdays were filled with school and lots of after school activities. I was just that kind of kid. I loved music, so I joined the band. I learnt the recorder; I think every child inflicted this on their parents in the 70s and 80s. That first sound that emanated from the plastic, or if your parents had money, wooden, instrument was enough to break glass.

It just escalated from there. I was one of those kids who practiced and practiced, until soon I was playing 'In an English Country Garden'. I couldn't wait to tell my long suffering parents that I had been given a chance to learn the treble; a bigger recorder that had a deeper tone. When I asked, Dad said yes, because he wanted us to do things that would educate us.

I came home from school carrying this treasure of the music world, I showed it around my family, letting them touch it and try to make a sound. Then I promptly rushed up to my room and began the squeak, toot, squeak.

Not satisfied with my launch into the instrument world, I searched for something else. Next came the choir, and another evening taken after school.

I wasn't the best singer in the world, but I could hold my own and whatever I lacked in talent, I made up for in enthusiasm. Again I was allowed to sing in front of the school at our assembly in the morning. A group of us stood up and floated angelically to the front and in harmony, well, a kind of harmony, we gave our unique rendition of 'All Things Bright and Beautiful'. Can you imagine our glee when we were informed by none other than the head teacher that we were going to do the song again at the end of term? And, wait for it, all our parents would be invited to this musical extravaganza.

I rushed home, floating on a cloud, eager to tell my parents the amazing news.

"Mum, Dad, guess what?" I dropped my bag and stood in the middle of the room, ready to make my epic announcement.

"You have found a golden ticket in a chocolate bar, now you get to see Willy Wonka's chocolate factory. We will all have chocolate for life." Dad rubbed his hands together.

"Dad, don't be silly, that's just a book." I wasn't amused. Well, maybe a little.

"So, no chocolate. That's ruined my day, Tracey." He pretended to look disappointed.

"Stop being silly, Arnold," said Mum. "What is it you have to tell us?"

I straightened up, really proud of what I was going to say, and I knew they were going to be as excited as me.

"I am going to be singing in the assembly, when the school shuts for holidays, and we can bring our parents as well."

Mum looked at Dad, who was rubbing his hands together, his lips tightening with embarrassment. "You know your Dad isn't well; it will make him ill walking to the school," she said.

We didn't have a car, and we didn't know anyone who did. So unless you walked to the destination, or got on a bus, you were stuck.

I didn't want my Dad to feel bad. He did what he could and I couldn't bear it if walking to school to see me made him ill. Like any typical child, sometimes you forget that your parents are getting older. I was born when they were a lot older than most parents so it was a little worse for me.

"It doesn't matter, Dad." I walked over to him and touched his hand. He looked up, sadness in his eyes. He ruffled my hair.

"Mum will go, curly tots," said Dad with a weak smile.

I always laughed when he called me that. His nickname had been Totts Holland, because of his curly black hair. Mine was tighter and red, and I had inherited the Totts from him. Dad had added the curly, just for me.

Mum did come on that special day to listen and when I got home, I stood in the middle of our living room, still in my pretty dress, and sang the same song, just for my dad.

"It's not the same, Dad, I couldn't bring all my friends to sing their parts." I laughed.

"You sang it for me, lass, and you sounded like an angel." He ruffled my hair again.

When I was ready to go to senior school, my participation in after school activities didn't stop. I was just as keen to involve myself in whatever was going on. You should have seen my parents' faces when I came home with a cornet. Not the one from an ice cream man, with a flake and strawberry sauce. It is similar to a trumpet but smaller and it was laid in a carrying case with blue velvet lining. Mum and Dad must have thought they were safe when the recorder playing had stopped, and then boom, a trumpet. I went to my bedroom to practise, leaving my parents still looking shocked. Janet took one look at the instrument and walked straight past me.

“I’m so glad I am getting married. Sharing a room with you is becoming bad for my health.” She started to walk down the stairs.

“Janet, you’ve forgotten something.” I laughed as I lifted the trumpet out of its case. “You haven’t got a house yet, so you and Billy will be living here. You may have this room, but I’ll be across from you in the little room and I’ll still be practising.”

Janet carried on down the stairs, not saying a word. I could imagine my mum, sister and dad, all sat downstairs, trying to think of a way to bury the trumpet in the back yard while I was asleep. It didn’t matter, though, as I was soon lost in the new sounds that I was making. Well, attempting to make without going blue and fainting.

Again, not content with the trumpet, I went in search of more, and that’s when I found the junior choir and the drama group. After my second week I came home to find Dad looking at me strangely.

“Hello, do I know you? I remember having a daughter called Tracey. She went to school last week and we haven’t seen her since.” He was laughing.

“Funny, Dad, you should have been a comedian; you would have made millions.” I sat on the settee and I had to admit I was a little tired.

In the drama group I started with small parts. I loved the stage; the acting, the lights, the props, just everything. I breathed it in and it became an important part of my life. I think my dad noticed this and he would ask me questions about what I was doing and how it was going. It gave us something we could share, and I treasured those moments that brought us closer.

Finally, in my fourth year at school, I was given the chance to act professionally at the Crucible Theatre in Sheffield. This was before it became famous for the snooker. The size of the part didn't worry me. Being able to act on a proper stage, with real actors and actresses, was a dream come true. When I told my family, Dad was over the moon and he couldn't wait to tell all the neighbours.

Dad couldn't walk far, but occasionally he felt good enough to slowly walk up the path. Mum would put a chair there and he would bask in the sun and chat to neighbours. The Manor Estate was like that. We were all in the same boat, with no money. Still, we always had time for one another and whatever we had we would gladly share if someone was in need.

Now my weekends became busy with rehearsals, as well as the other commitments I had. It was great meeting the actors and actresses and we would ask them all sorts of things about how they became famous. The only thing that took the shine out of all my dreams of being on the stage was my dad not being able to see me. I knew he was ill, but this was one thing I really wanted him to be a part of.

We didn't talk about it. I could see he was upset, so instead I would talk about what the stage would look like and where I would be standing and what I would be wearing. I would go upstairs at night and cry. I wouldn't do it in front of my dad. I hated how cruel the world was and how someone as good as him could be inflicted with such an unfair illness. I cried because my life was just a set of pictures in his head and none could really be shared with him, not in a full measure anyway.

On the day of my first performance I arrived early in the afternoon. I couldn't stay at home as I couldn't bear the thought of not sharing this with my entire family. Janet and my mum were coming and Janet said she would take pictures, but it wasn't the same. I sat in the dressing room with the rest of my group and I had never felt so alone. All this would be nothing without Dad and my heart had a hole so big in it that it could have held the whole world.

I sat in the dressing room taking in the scent of paint and wood, with voices all animated and excited flowing all around me. This was something big for a teenager, the stuff dreams were made of, and my only wish was for an ill parent to witness it.

Then it was time to go on and we were bustled to the corridors under the stage that led up a ramp then out into a circle in front of our audience. I was ushered on, and up I went into the lights and into my position. The scene started. I can't say I remember much, there were voices and lights, the scent of leather seats, and then we were off. As I filed down the ramp I glanced up to the seats I knew my family were in. Then everything slowed, time stopped and everything centred on the person sat next to Mum.

My dad. My dad was there sitting in the seat, with a big smile on his face, all his pain gone in the moment our eyes met. He had seen me on stage, once, and I knew this was something special for him. I knew he had fought the pain and got here for his little girl and I loved him so much I wanted to shout to everyone.

"Look – my dad!"

I don't think anyone had ever felt as much joy as I did, one small girl just outside the lights of that enormous stage, sharing a glance with her father.

The rest of the evening was the best ever, and when it was finished and the final light went down, we all ran on stage. I stood there, not watching the audience, just my dad, who I found out later on had got a taxi and slowly made his way into his seat and sat through the pain with an endurance beyond what was normal. And even though he said I was a superstar, I feel he was the star and his performance was faultless.

The West Pier
By Kimberly Jamison

The West Pier
is a wooden spider.
It is the
arsonist's artistry.
The wind blows through
the gaping rooftop spine
but the concert hall
stays silenced.
Its legs are splayed,
determined to remain,
dipping its cast-iron toes
into the murky sea,
pointing to the place
someone swam to
to light the flame
that turned a postcard picture
into this
burnt out ruin.

London, Home
By Sara Assumani

Have you ever wondered what comes after death? Heaven? Hell? A dark abyss of nothingness? A sky like this, so brilliant and crepuscular that it beckons at a glance, and takes our souls into infinity?

Emma
By Sanjana Parikh

"YOU ASSHOLE! THAT WAS MY MOTHER'S GIFT TO ME!"

The wooden patio was where Emma sat all day and listened to the noise that rattled the house. She hid her face between her knees and tried to think of happy times. But were there any? She waited for the bad moment to pass. The wind gently stroked her champagne coloured hair and she rubbed her deep blue eyes. Her parents' fighting had woken her up early. She heard a few glasses smash against the wall from her their room, so she sleepily got up and went downstairs. The sun had not emerged yet. She couldn't see anything in the dark, just like she couldn't see where she was going in her life. It was quiet outside, just like it was always quiet for her. She hardly paid attention to anything or anyone around her. The fighting had now shifted to the living room downstairs.

She was used to the swearing now. It was quite recently that her Mother told her that her Father had never wanted her. When she had gotten pregnant, he had tried to force her to get an abortion, but she was adamant.

"He had always hated children, Emma. There was a time when I wanted kids, but my priorities have changed now. You will not expect anything out of me and as long as you live under our roof, you will do exactly what we tell you to, without asking any questions."

Emma did not mind making food and cleaning the floors. She did not mind being restricted from doing her homework or skipping school few times for that matter. The only thing that bothered her was when her Father had asked her to 'satisfy' friends of his. The pain had been unbearable, but he had kept his hand over her mouth to stop her from screaming. She was nine, then.

After everyone had gone to sleep that night, Emma slowly climbed down the wooden stairs inside the house, but her Father had not repaired the broken steps. Emma fell face down on the ground and, unfortunately, he had been sleeping in the living room that night. He had grabbed her by the arm and locked her in the attic for three days, without food. She learned at that very moment that it would be impossible to run away from this life.

"YOU'RE A FUCKING MORON," her Mom shouted again, and Emma was pulled back to the present, but only for a moment.

Her mind started playing her kindergarten teacher's voice. For a second, it felt like she was speaking from a distance, but then the memory was clear like the volume had been turned up.

"Jamie, would you please tell me a word starting with the letter F?"

"Um…"

"Fuck," Emma said before Jamie could even think of anything.

That day, her parents had been called in, and when confronted, they acted like they had no idea where she had picked up the word. When they returned home, Emma had been slapped twice on her cheek for disgracing her parents.

She laughed as she opened her eyes. Her mind always wandered off into space, reminding her of her dreadful childhood. She was five when she had received the first blow from her Father. She had puked on the floor and he had made her clean it while her Mother watched.

Her parents considered her a liability. She realized soon enough that nothing she did was appreciated because they never wanted her in the first place. She had been going through this for 14 years now, and she was exhausted. Her parents were not well off at all, and that worsened the scenario. Emma had no friends, no one to confide in, no one to rely upon, no one to laugh with; basically, no one in her life. Sitting outside made no difference, so she decided to get up and go to her room.

As she stepped inside the house, she froze. She could feel the bile rising in the back of her throat as she looked at her Mother who lay on the floor, crying, drops of blood around her. Her Father was standing over her, whispering angrily to his wife. Emma could barely make out what he was saying.

"You are a burden. Your daughter is a burden. I would love to kill you both." He felt her eyes upon him.

"What the hell you starin' at?"

Emma ran upstairs to her room. She pushed the door open just to see a friend of her Father lying naked on her bed.

"I've been waitin' for you." He smiled seductively.

Emma ran to the terrace. She had had enough. Her parents did not want her, fair enough, but she was tired of them making her do things she did not want to do. She was no whore. Tears started rolling down her eyes, tears that hadn't come in these 14 years. A classmate at school had told her that she should pray to God and ask Him for happiness and that He always listened to prayers. She prayed, all day every day. He never answered... clearly. She had hit her saturation point now. She didn't believe in God anymore, rather, she didn't believe in the concept of God.

Emma walked to the edge of the terrace and climbed over the railing. She gazed at the now blue sky, the sun slowly rising up to shine at everyone but her. It was a new day, a fresh start, but not for her. She felt betrayed, humiliated, used and hopeless. She knew right then, what she had to do.

When I Grow Up
By Natasha Keates

The trees entwined, curving around a view of the autumn countryside.
A dusty mirror's glimmer of sun beamed through the cove.
Pictures taken of our friends running around the grounds, rolling down hills.

When he climbed up the tree and couldn't get down.
How we struggled through a ditch instead of taking the path.
The boys catching the girls as they jumped down,
Pushing them up the steep wall of grass and mud.

We mocked the statues,
Imitated them.
Laughed at the naked man clinging to a bed sheet,
At the adults proclaiming "It's art!"

Children walked alongside their parents,
Looking up at us.

We still ran through the empty fountain,
Pointed at the early moon in awe,
Gave voices to the nearby deer.

Stumbling home,
Our arms linked into each other as the couples and grandparents looked down at us.
Shielded their children from us.

Although the cold nibbled at our toes,
We danced through the mud.

And we asked the chilly wind to blow,
For then the trees can dance as well.

The Chair
By Elisa Gradwohl

No one had visited this place for a while, that much was obvious. Dust coated the furniture and floors like soot covered Pompeii. Grandma wouldn't have been pleased if she saw how her house was now. She always kept it radiantly clean. Besides working, Grandma spent her days cooking, cleaning, and napping in the old rocking chair, being fairly pleasant unless she was woken up. I sat there, in her dark abandoned house, across from her favourite spot, remembering the countless times I stayed in this house. Grandma's house was always open to family, but I certainly visited the most. I loved to give her hugs, breathing in her scent; the heavy perfume and faint trace of tobacco. As I sat there remembering the person I loved and respected the most, I heard something that made my heart stop.

"What do you want, boy?" My head snapped up. There, sitting in her rocking chair, was my grandmother, making it creak and groan as she swayed it back and forth gently. This would have been normal, if she hadn't died six months ago sending me spiralling into a depression I had just begun to crawl out of.

"Well? Why'd you wake me up? I haven't got all day!"

Sparse Horizon
By Kaya Gromocki

Taken in Alderly Edge, Cheshire

Freedom.
By Andrea Bowd

I can see fronds
beneath
translucent ice,
like hair,
pulled straight with
the flow of the fast,
dark water.
I can feel the fronds
waving, screaming,
hiding white mouths.
Lips opening and closing
with the ebb and flow.
If I listen closely,
a limb might appear
and break a fist shaped hole
through the cold blanket.

Amsterdam
By Liam Powell

The silver bird touched down,
lightly, on the foreign tarmac.
Teenage faces were nervous,
confident and wary.

Everybody knew,
yet nobody knew,
what happens in Amsterdam.

Seven lads dressed up,
and hit the town.
Every street was a snapshot,
the city was a picture book.

The heart of the diamonds,
the heart of the drugs,
so much of the good,
and so much of the bad.

Everybody knew,
yet nobody knew,
what happens in Amsterdam.

Friday night went further on.
The haze wasn't given a second thought.
Fifty Euros of pleasure stood
on every street corner.

Everybody knows,
yet nobody knows,
what happens in Amsterdam.

Hare Series 1 – Untitled #1
By Lydia Crump

Tidying
By Matthew Lewis Miller

There's a piece of pale blue plastic on my desk. It could be a little blue plastic dolphin if you squinted, if you thought hard. Useless. I could put it in the drawer. I should throw it out. But to move it would be to acknowledge it, would be a step towards organisation that would need to be followed by another step, and another step. And when my room is tidy, what then? Must I move onto the kitchen, the living room, the stairs, my childhood, my mind? I don't know where the hoover is kept and there's work to be done. Now…

But for all I hobble myself to my laptop screen, surrounded by littered forget-me-nots, my brain crawls like a monkey out through my nasal cavity to examine the blue plastic dolphin lying on its side. I call my monkey back. It will not come. The dolphin grins at me. Its deep and trough-like grin. I reach out a hand and brush it aside to create space. It rolls up to the sellotape. They link arms and chuckle. I call my monkey back. It crawls back into my skull. It tries to work. Tries to play. But the dolphin is blubbering yowls and it will not stop. My monkey covers my ears with its palms.

Regret
By Sean Keenan

It's just past midnight as you wake up and head down the compact corridor to the bathroom. You figure there's no point in turning on the light; you're too old to be afraid of the dark. As you wash your hands, you glance up at the reflection staring back at you in the mirror.

It's not yours.

Two Can Play At That Game
By Helen Raven

"You're what?"

"I'm breaking up with you."

Sean Dobson sits across from me, dressed in his smarmy designer suit, with his dark curls brushed to the side, his beautiful high cheek bones and cool blue eyes. He looks angry, but I've made my decision. He leans forward on the table.

"So let me get this straight," he says. "You want to break up?" he asks, a frown passing across his handsome face.

I nod. "Yes."

"Why?" he asks. "Is there someone else?"

"No," I say, resisting the urge to roll my eyes.

"Then what's going on?"

"You see, the thing is," I start. "I don't know what I want right now. There is so much more I want to do with my life before I settle down." I look at him and reach across the table for his hand, but he moves it away.

"I don't understand, Jasmine," he says. "Three weeks ago you tell me you want to take a break. I didn't argue, I took a step back and gave you some space and now you're telling me you want to break up?"

"You have a great, successful job, Sean. You're ready to settle down, get married and have kids. I just don't think I'm ready for that right now!"

"Then we'll wait," he says, shrugging and sitting back. He takes a sip from his pint of bitter before speaking again. "I'm in no rush. We'll wait 'til you're ready."

"No," I say, glancing down at my untouched Mojito, my favourite drink. "No, Sean. I don't want to get back together."

I can't read the expression that paints itself on his face. "You don't want to get back together?" he repeats.

One nil to me. I nod, trying so hard not to smile. "That's right."

He stands up. "Then you can pay for your own drink."

I watch as he walks over to the bar to settle his tab. He doesn't look back as he storms out. Glancing down at the menu, my eyes widen and I whistle at the prices. This is not the best place to break up with someone.

I guess I deserve that one. Nice one, jerk. One all.

Later that evening, I get back home to my cosy little studio flat and I can't help but smile, despite the events of the evening. I switch the lights on and I feel like a whole weight has lifted now that I've broken up with Sean. I don't need a fancy apartment with a balcony view over the whole city to make me happy. I love my little studio flat; it's the main reason why I always refused to move in with Sean whenever he asked. This is all I need. Heading straight to my bedroom, I take off my jacket and put it over my chair. I take my heels off and throw them down, onto the pile of other shoes I own in the corner of my room. Oscar, my adorable sheepdog, comes bounding forward to greet me having heard me come in. I kneel down and hug him.

‘Hello, boy,’ I say, losing my hands in his fur as I stroke him. He licks at my face joyfully. Another reason why I’d never move in with Sean. His place is a fancy and posh with an en suite and a balcony, and he doesn’t like mess and he definitely doesn’t like dogs. I’d have to give up Oscar, and that’s never happening.

I pull away from Oscar and peel off my clothes, deciding to change into something a little more comfortable to lounge around in. I leave my dress on the bed and pull on my large hoodie and pyjama bottoms before slipping my feet into my favourite pair of slipper socks. I go over to my dressing table and look at myself in the mirror. Scooping my hair up into a ponytail, I secure it with a bobble from around my wrist.

With Oscar at my heel, I walk back into the other room, heading for the kitchen area. A mug of hot chocolate with marshmallows and huge bar of chocolate from my secret stash sounds perfect right about now. I can practically hear it calling out to me. Oscar follows me around, sniffing and barking every now again, showing his excitement in seeing me home.

Ten minutes later, I’m snuggled up on the sofa with a blanket and Oscar’s head resting on my lap. I have my mug of hot chocolate in my hands, my chocolate bar the other side of me, out of reach for Oscar. The television is on, and I’m watching my favourite movie *The Holiday* even though it’s not Christmas.

At about eleven thirty there’s a knock on the door. I reach forward and put my empty mug onto the coffee table. I pause the DVD and shift Oscar’s head as I try and stand up; he growls in surprise, but still shuffles over to his own basket. I head for the door and look through the peep hole, surprised to see Sean standing there on my door step. I open the door.

“Sean,” I say, greeting him. “This isn’t on your way home.”

Sean looks at me, his eyes bleary and red, as if he's been crying.

"Please, Jas, I'm sorry. Can I come in?"

I step back to let him by. He walks in and stops at the kitchen counter, looking around my flat.

"Why are you here?" I ask, folding my arms.

He turns to face me. "Please," he says. "Don't do this, let's not break up. I love you."

"Sean..." I sigh.

He walks over and slips his arms around my waist and kisses me lightly on the lips. He lingers, and I can smell a strong whiff of alcohol but there's that familiar scent, which has already weakened my defences. He pulls back. "We're good together, you know that, and I promise I won't rush you into anything you don't want to do..." He leans in again and plants another lingering kiss, this time more passionate, as if he means what he's saying.

I feel my legs weaken and I know I'm going to cave in. His lips leave mine and he starts kissing me along my collarbone and up my neck, where he knows I like it. I sigh in ecstasy, and I kiss him back, pushing my hands into his darks curls. He picks me up and carries me over to the sofa, pulling my hoodie over my head at the same time. My hands start to unbutton his shirt. It feels right and in that moment of passion, I realize that I don't want to lose him. We'll make things work between us...

The next morning, I wake up and my bed is empty. I sit up, propping myself on my elbows. I look around my bedroom.

The curtains are closed but the sun is streaming against them, desperate to get in.

"Sean?" I call out.

There's no answer.

"Sean?" I try again.

With a sigh, I roll out of bed, putting on my robe. He's probably using the bathroom. I go out into the other room. Oscar is snoring lightly in his basket, having not been disturbed. I check the bathroom, knocking quietly on the door before I go in. He's not there. I go back out into the living area. His clothes are gone from the floor by the sofa, where he left them last night. I stand there. He's gone. And that makes me angry. I was going to give our relationship a second chance. I thought that's what he had wanted. I can't believe I fell for it. I let out a cry of rage and thump my fist against the counter. That's when I see the note. I pick it up and read Sean's familiar scrawl.

Two can play at that game, bitch. I win.

Two one. Well played.

2 Minds
By Uta Feinstein

The Legion of Dark Angels
By Sara Assumani

Prologue

A faint latching sound ticked in the far distance.

What would have been inaudible to the human ear was loud enough to fire Rex's senses. Instinct drove her as she sprinted across the cobbled road, and swiftly slid across a car hood. She ducked beside the wheel just as a razor sharp arrow flew through the car window and past the tip of her ear, lodging itself into the brick wall behind.

"Amateurs," she muttered.

Rex patted her pockets to see if she had anything that she could construct into a weapon, but she had nothing but a silver coin. Ears trained on her target, Rex shot up just as the brave soul stepped out into the street. She flipped the coin into the air, and performed a powerful roundhouse kick. The force sent the coin spinning directly towards the Catcher's skull, embedding itself deeply between his eyes. *Bingo, one down before he could even aim his motherfucking crossbow.*

"Why don't you come out and fight me with honour, chicken shit?" Rex called out as she lowered herself back down.

A deep rumbling voice called back, "I'm not falling for that one, you crazy bitch!"

"Here's what I'll do," she called back, ignoring his unoriginality. "I won't kill you."

The man scoffed. "Am I *really* supposed to believe that? You just killed Stanis!"

Rex recognized the name of the Catcher and held back a snicker. She had always thought that he was a stupid liability; too brave and too proud for his own good. She figured then, that she knew exactly whom she was addressing, and rolled her eyes.

"Angus?"

"And if it is?" he growled. He was so annoying.

Rex sighed, "Send Mercury my love. I'm not coming back." She stood up then, and dragged a hand through her short spiked pixie cut. "And you won't kill me."

"I wouldn't be so sure." The man emerged from the darkness of the trees. His thick blonde hair was slicked back to his neck, and his eyes, a watery, powerful blue glared at Rex with accusation.

"Traitor bitch," he spat on the ground.

The sound of Rex's boots slapping against the floor echoed as she made her way to meet him in the middle. She stood, directly facing him, fiercely decked out in skin hugging black jeans that were ripped at the knees, a pair of black, vintage, sturdy Doc Martens and a very expensive looking black leather jacket. Beside him, Rex was significantly smaller at five foot four. Her short and shiny hair was so dark that it almost glinted blue in the evening light. In an ordinary situation, Rex's size would have been humorous, but the dangerous look on her face and the readiness of her posture radiated skilled menace. Her cheekbones were prominent on her heart-shaped face, her eyes like supernovas and black diamonds. She was hauntingly beautiful.

Reaching into her pocket, Rex casually pulled out a pack of Marlboro and lit up a cigarette. She took a puff, but before she could blow, Angus smacked it out of her hand. She easily deflected his assault and kicked him so fast at his knee that the joint dislocated and brought him crumbling down to the ground. Rex grabbed him by the neck and growled as she began to crush his bones slowly, eyes bright in fury.

“I’m not coming back.”

“You’re one of us,” he choked violently. His features were morphed into an expression of complete agony, “deep inside, you know...”

As quickly as she grabbed him, Rex let go and allowed him to slump down. Her exterior betrayed no emotion; her eyes held no compassion, no empathy, no feeling.

“I’m whatever I want to be.” She whipped around and drew up her hood.

Rex was racing down the dark street. The light of the moon trailed her, and shadows curled around her feet as though they belonged there. Finally reaching her slick, black *IZH 2012 Hybrid*, Rex leapt onto the motorbike and pumped the gas, accelerating off into the distance and far away from any more Catchers that threatened to take her back to the Legion.

Bandits

By Kimberly Jamison

The silhouette could barely be made out in the moonlight against the dark backdrop of the deep navy sky. It was a starless night and fog had settled, casting an eerie atmosphere for any unfortunate traveller that happened to walk past. This was a dangerous place and these were dangerous times. Bandits roamed the woods. Some of them, however, were far more sinister than petty thieves. They had only plans for revenge on their minds. The locals feared to walk close to the forests even during hours of sunlight; however, the tax collector the king had sent from the capital was not to know this. He was new to these parts. He would learn the hard way.

He sat upon his stagecoach, diligently gripping the reins. The horses were acting up more than usual. Something had spooked them about a mile back. He had chosen to travel down the edge of the forest because it sheltered him somewhat from the harsh February winds. Suddenly leaf and plant debris blew out onto the path, the nervous horses reared. He took his eyes off the road for a moment, just a moment to pull the reins back and regain control. That was the moment they needed.

As soon as he looked back, there was a hooded figure standing in the undergrowth of the forest. The figure lifted his head and the lunar glow outlined his face. It was haunting; his cheekbones hollowed out and his eyes had dilated so much they were a pool of blackness. He may have been human but there was something equally demonic about him. Before the tax collector realized, he had been surrounded by another four hooded men.

"Stand and deliver!" the figure ordered, holding a bow and arrow aimed at the tax man's head. The tax collector pulled out his sword from under the rug he had laid on his seat. He had been trained for this. With one jump he was on the ground and he lurched towards one of the bandits. He moved silently and impossibly quickly. The tax collector stabbed at thin air, then felt a crushing blow to the back of his head. He swivelled round as he fell and swiped outwards with the blade and caught his assailant on the shoulder. The man barely flinched. The tax man writhed in agony. The bandit turned back to the coach, knowing the man he had just injured wouldn't pose any more threat.

The tax collector's mind was now in panic, maybe it had just been a flesh wound, or maybe he didn't even hit him. His only thoughts were on the contents of the coach. He hadn't only been carrying the taxes. The king had entrusted him to bring him deeds that could potentially dethrone him. If anyone got a hold of them, especially the bandits, the country could be in ruins. The tax man started to recognize them from their wanted posters and acts of treason. By now the imperial guards inside the coach had jumped out, no doubt they had been asleep. They were in full on arm to arm combat. The king's men outnumbered these expert highwaymen yet somehow they seemed to be fighting on the losing side. It wasn't superior fighting ability that they were fighting against; they just seemed to be *quicker.* The knights couldn't hit them.

The injury to his head was agonising. As his breathing swallowed, everything seemed to start spinning. He could feel the blood spilling from his head, staining his livery scarlet. There was one last thing he could do. The horses couldn't bolt the same way because the coach was too heavy, weighted down due to the preciousness of the cargo that they couldn't afford to lose. The collector hauled himself up the slope to where they had run. He dragged himself to the coach. He had to dodge the horses that were rearing out of control. Pulling himself up to the window, he reached inside to find the wooden torch that they used to patrol the villages and lit it. He threw it out at the bandits who now had defeated all the guards who were now lying worryingly still on the ground. They scattered. High pitched screeches and wails came from them. The blaze caught the dead wood on the ground and the flames began to get higher.

He looked around; his vision was now one continuous blur. He managed to focus enough to grab onto one of the horses. He hit it, signalling to run and they charged as fast as the coach would let them. The horse was extremely startled by the fire and reared up in fright but it had been trained well and eventually did what it was told after the signal. There were arms trying to pull him off the horse but they disappeared as soon as the horses charged off. He felt a sharp pain in his arm but didn't have the energy to look round to see what it was.

The chief bandit lowered his bow. He had hit his target but it hadn't stopped the coach. He had a cruel grin on his thin face. They had waited years; they could wait even more to enact their revenge. They knew exactly what was contained in the deeds the coach held and exactly how to use them. He had found anyone in the king's court could be treacherous if they gave enough money. He and his men were not going to let this opportunity slip through their hands; they had a cause after all.

He watched the coach drive into the distance. He wasn't worried, he had men stationed every few miles and anyway, the chase was his favourite part...

Eyeland
By Keira Andrews

There is a place that you visit every time you fall asleep, and the moment you wake up, you forget you ever went. For some, it's a little village that floats in the sea. Whilst for others, the little houses are hidden in dark caves, and each village is full of little people who grow by the day.

These people, who call themselves Dolrins, have known everything about you since the day you were born. The world that you visit when you shut your eyes each night is completely unique – nobody, but you, can venture to those forgotten isles.

This is the story about a little boy, named Jacob, who had eyes the colour of a garden pond. The Dolrins that lived in Jacob's world had heads the shape of a sideways rugby ball, and they walked through the village with a skip in their step. The Dolrins all live in the fabled, green land of Eyeland.

And, if you were to travel by bird, pig, or sheep over the grassy hills of Jacob's Eyeland, you would find fields upon fields of broccoli-coloured crops.

You would see how the scarecrows are made completely out of lime, and you would laugh at the steps made from the skins of a watermelon. If you were lucky, very lucky indeed, you might catch sight of the avocado-bear – a fearful beast that can only roll sideways as it searches for a meal that isn't the slightest bit green.

But amongst it all, if you were looking closely, you might get a glimpse of a small village with a hand-painted sign, reading 'Iriston'. And if you land on a visit to the world, you would spot that most of the small houses were just rubble and stone; awaiting a time when it was right for them to be built.

You would also notice how the castle turrets leant a little too far to the right, and that all the houses were made from the stems of a plant, all bundled together and covered with large, bright leaves.

On each door you would read a crooked notice, revealing the House's name, and you would use the doorknob made from a skinless kiwi fruit. Inside the olive-coloured rooms, you would meet those little Dolrins, all of them the very same height; around the size of a six year old who was nearing a birthday.

These little people are a sight to behold; their hair is a mess of reddish-brown curls and their skin is the palest shade of grey.

The Dolrins have three eyes; the left eye is the colour of the sky on a cloud-free day, their middle eye is as bright as an orange in the fruit bowl, and their right eye is the colour of chocolate cakes in a mudslide. Each eye blinks one at a time, and every blink is from a different direction.

All of the Dolrins work in Houses, and these little Houses have a character of their own. If, for example, you stood too long outside the House of Humour then the leafy rooftop would curl into a pipe and squirt you with rainwater until you walked away. And all you'd hear would be the peals of Dolrins' laughter as you catch a glimpse of them rolling across the floor, clutching their sides as they chuckle uncontrollably.

The House of Knowledge is to the north of Eyeland, and entry is only permitted if you answer the riddle correctly. If you fail, then the plant stems will form a prison and you'll stay there until you've learnt from your mistake.

It's here where the most serious of Dolrins like to work. Each bookcase is full of upside-down maps, and charts of observation. A large table, made from spinach leaves, fills the centre of the room – many Dolrins in white coats stand round it, and like to mutter, and utter, the most nonsensical of remarks.

The House of Imagination was built at the other end of the village, and it is by far the most unpredictable of them all. The front door will only appear if you think really hard, and the roof has a habit of flapping its sides in an attempt to learn how to fly.

In here, you would be more likely to see a Dolrin riding a pretend seahorse, or a talking flamingo instructing a dance routine.

Unlike the other houses in Jacob's Iriston, this house had two floors, and every hour a Dolrin would climb up the pole, way into the sky, and sit on a moss covered perch where they'd spend their time with their heads in the clouds.

But enough of that now; the snores from the castle are about to vibrate, and the whistling greenflies are beginning to whistle. It means it's time for a certain young boy to discover a world that has been waiting for this very day.

All the Dolrins, at this very moment, are clamouring out of their houses to line the village as they look to the sky, where a very big woman is peering down at the grassy hills as she says goodnight.

For up high, above the water dome that covers the land, a boy named Jacob is settling into bed. Jacob, with his untameable brown, curly hair and dark green eyes, feels a shiver of excitement and a sense of unease.

Unbeknownst to Jacob, the little Dolrins inside his eye are telling him to prepare, for the eve of a seventh birthday is quite the extraordinary affair.

The Fight
By Liam Powell

So there it is. The world's dumbest idea, now formalized into a full on battle plan. Nice one, lads.

My idiot little brother, Dom, as expected, puts himself right in the middle of it all. Him and his friends – Joey, Ryan, Billy, whoever else – are taking on the hard nut of the school. They say that anyway. Act like big men now, when they see him they'll run a mile. The name alone is enough to tell anyone that this guy is not to be messed with: Brian Little.

It's like a scene from Rocky. School kids everywhere; some riding on bikes with hoods up trying to look tough (personally, I think they looked like divs), others on the outskirts looking excited, though terrified that Brian Little may suddenly turn on them. Dom and his mates are loving it; lapping up the attention, it's going to be them to end the terror of Brian. Yeah, right, good luck with that one, boys. Everybody's waiting, and what will they do when Brian finally comes out and sees this fuss? Maybe one or two might leave early after all.

Here we go. Somebody quite huge is on their way over. Left and right he's looking, scowling all the while. He doesn't exactly look thrilled. Dom and his little friends aren't looking amused anymore, but scared. They know they're in trouble now. Yep, there they go. Mr Bean – the most ferocious, yet intelligent, Head of Science you could ever come across – frog marching Dom, Joey, Ryan and Billy back into the school. The whole yard's wetting themselves.

Never let Dom forget this.

I Sit Here.
By Kwaku Asafu-Agyei

I sit here trapped in a whirlwind
of time; so many commotions
in the sea, leaving people anxious.

I sit here trapped in a world where
there is a lot to be done. Where
some people tell lies to get to the
top.

I sit here fascinated with nature;
just watching the birds fly. The
sun shine, and the trees sway
from side to side.

I sit here reminiscing about
my past trying to figure
out how I can make my future
better for me and the human race.

I sit here listening to music that
soothes my soul; makes me dream
that I have made it to the other side,
Heaven.

Where there is no pain; no heartache
just nothing but peace.
I dream of this
place while my thoughts begin to flow.
I sit here.

Untitled (2)
By Uta Feinstein

The Yellow Plastic Bike
By Tracey Holland
An excerpt from the memoirs, 'Born in the Change'.

"Tracey, what have you done?"

I turned to my mum, who was looking very angry and red faced. I was scared, so I threw myself to the floor in my typical drama queen way and started to cry.

My sister, Janet, was sitting on the sofa, rubbing her head and looking a little dazed. Mum sat down next to her and began to examine the large lump that had begun to grow like a second head above her eye.

Mum turned her full gaze on me, and pointing her finger, yelled, "You've really hurt your sister; I should smack you for this."

My reply was to cry even louder.

Janet moved my mum to one side and stood up, wobbling slightly. She tried to stop her, but Janet pulled out of her grasp. She came over to me and lowered herself until she was sitting at my side, then she enveloped me in her thin arms.

"It's ok, Tracey, see I was not hurt." She smiled and tapped her head to prove her point. "I must be made of concrete." She laughed.

"So is someone going to tell me what happened?" Mum stared at the pair of us.

I was the first to answer. "I wanted Jan Jan to play with me." I showed her my new yellow bike lying on its side at the end of the sofa.

It had been a recent gift, and I was so excited. Trouble was, my little legs didn't quite reach the pedals, so I needed some help to get it started. And to be truthful, patience was not in my DNA.

"But Jan Jan wouldn't listen, she had her eyes shut, so I got angry." I stopped; knowing what I said next would get me the slap my mum had promised earlier. And unlike my dad, who slapped us on the legs, where the sound was louder than the pain, Mum knew exactly where to slap me and make it count.

"Then what, Tracey?" Mum was determined to get to the truth. She stood there still and staring. I knew I could not get away with this, even if I was the youngest and smallest.

I turned to Janet and saw how much the lump had grown. I reached out and touched it, and it was hot, her skin stretching to allow it to get bigger. My sister had tears in her eyes, I realized then how much I had hurt her. I put my small arms around her, they didn't fit, but I tried, then I began to cry again.

"Mum, I hit Jan Jan with the scooter."

We were so different, Janet and I. There was the twelve year age gap to start with, but even if you didn't take that into account, we were total opposites.

Janet had been born with two holes in her heart and was a sickly child. Everything was an effort for her. Still I remember her strength and total determination. She fought for a normal life and was not going to be left behind. School was hard, but she was allowed to come home at dinnertime to rest. The thing was I wanted her attention and she then went without that needed rest.

I was fiery to her placid, excitable to her calm, yet we always seemed to somehow meet in the middle. One thing we did share was our interest in the world around us and books. We were always reading, either on our own, or to one another.

When I was 4 we moved to the Manor, to Cullabine road. That's when the area was nice and we had the Lord Mayor of Sheffield living at the top of the road. I remember I used to take his dogs for walks and he'd pay me 50p. That was enough for a couple of magazines and some sweets. It's something Dad always encouraged, so I did that and had a paper round.

Me and my sister shared the front room, and it was huge. The best thing about it was the old iron fire in the corner. On cold winter's nights, Dad would light the fire and the whole room would be flooded with amber flickering lights. We would sit on the floor in front of it and toast bread. Mum would bring us two plates with a knob of butter and jam on the edge. I don't know why, but toast made this way always seemed to taste better. We would sit there cross legged, munching toast and watching the fire cast dancing shadows on the walls.

We both adored our father, probably because we spent more time with him. Mum worked a lot, to keep the house going. Dad, being the disabled one, became the house Dad. He knew our weaknesses well, so our punishments always fitted our crimes. I would have to say mine more so, as Janet was usually well behaved and too weak to cause much trouble, but she did have her moments.

I was always reading, the trouble was getting me to stop. When I was reading I was in another world, especially if the book was a fantasy. To be taken away and allowed to travel in your mind to these places excited me. I would build the scene in my mind and would feel as though they were taking me with them. I was one of the children in Narnia, and I knew personally Mr Tumnus and Aslan. The characters became my friends and extended family. I pulled them into my world and they lived with me every day.

Janet was the same. Her world was so small, that books allowed her the freedom to roam through the places contained within the pages. She could travel to exotic places, climbing hills and trekking through jungles that in the real world would destroy her body. We also loved music, especially the old MGM musical and Rodgers and Hammerstein. We were unusual kids, but I think it was because our parents were elderly; we came to appreciate a broader set of tastes.

When Janet left school, she was determined to work, even though the Doctors said it could be dangerous. She became a shop assistant at the Co-op that was just down the road and in walking distance from the house. Everyone liked her and she soon got a promotion into the office. That's when the boyfriends came along, and I was not happy. They wanted my Jan Jan's attention and like a typical child I played up. Until my Dad took me to one side and told me it could be fun. I couldn't see how, but Dad told me to sit between Janet and her latest boyfriend and watch what happened. I wasn't convinced, but I decided to give it a try.

There was a knock at the door and in came Aiden, Janet's latest conquest. He said hello to us all and sat on the settee to wait for Janet. I heard footsteps on the stairs, it was Janet. As she came through the door, she saw Aiden and smiled. Dad beckoned her to sit down and talk a bit before they left. Dad turned and winked at me and when Janet sat next to Aiden, I went and sat between them. The strange thing was both Aiden and Janet frowned at me. Dad got up to make a drink and we were left alone in the room.

"Tracey, I thought you said you were going to your room to read."

"No, I can do that later."

"How about helping Dad with the tea?"

"Can't touch the kettle, mum says it's too hot."

"Do you like sweets?" said Aiden, putting his hand in his pocket and pulling out a fifty pence piece.

I smiled at Aiden until my cheeks hurt. I grabbed the 50p, thinking this was something I definitely needed to remember.

When Janet got to 19 the doctors told her she needed an operation on her heart. I wasn't keen on hospitals and didn't like the idea of my poorly sister there. Mum and Dad sat down and tried to explain.

"You know Jan Jan has holes in her heart?" Dad said quietly.

"Yes, Dad, that's what makes her sleepy." I smiled back, because I had remembered. My family did not hide much from us children. I think it brought us together and made us stronger. I knew even though I was little, I had to help Janet; I wanted to be a part of it.

But when Janet went in the hospital, fiery Tracey reappeared.

"When can I see Jan Jan?" I was missing her so much.

"You will see her when she comes home." Mum didn't look at me when she said it, and I wasn't won, not one bit.

"Why can't I see her now? You and Dad can." I wasn't getting the answer I wanted.

Dad laughed and patted on the settee for me to join him.

“Janet has had a serious operation and she is in a special part of the hospital. And only grown-ups can go there.” Dad ruffled my red curls.

I didn’t say anything, I needed to go and think. So I went upstairs and sat on my bed. It wasn’t fair. My brother Arnold was grown up, so he could go. It wasn’t my fault I was little and that mum and dad had me late. If I told the nurses this they may change their minds. So I got a pen and paper and wrote.

> *Dear Nurses and Doctors.*
>
> *I really miss my sister, who shares my room. It is not nice without her.*
>
> *Thank you for making her better. I don’t think it’s fair that I can't come and see her because I am small. If I promise to be really good and quiet, please can I come and see her. This will make her better.*
>
> *Tracey Dawn Holland.*

I showed my dad the letter and he showed it to mum. They both started laughing, but Dad said he would give my letter to the doctor at the hospital. They would read it and decide.

A few days later dad was surprised when the doctor told him that I could see my sister. When dad had explained the age difference the doctor had said it would settle both of us, as Janet had asked to see me too. I decided to wear one of my best dresses. This was a bit of a revelation as I hated dresses, and would do anything to get out of wearing one. I wanted to look nice and show the doctors I was a good girl, then I would be allowed to visit more.

The hospital smelled funny and the people in the beds looked sad. I smiled a lot, hoping this would cheer them up. It must have worked as some smiled back and waved. I knew coming to the hospital was a good idea. I think they needed to be visited by more children; we made everyone happy.

Janet's bed was in a separate room and I stood in the doorway.

"Are you coming in?" Janet whispered.

I wasn't sure now. Janet looked so small and her face was grey, her hair limply hanging down her face. I felt scared, my poor Jan Jan was hurting, I knew it. I remembered when I hit her with the scooter, the red, warm lump and the sadness in her face. I didn't know what to do and I didn't like this plain white, smelly room, I didn't like the doctors and nurses who had hurt her and I didn't like the plastic tubes sticking out of her and the machines that beeped and flashed. So I burst into tears.

"Come here, you pudding," Janet said, opening her arms for me to run to.

I dashed towards her then stopped.

"It's ok; I am stronger than you think."

My small arms didn't fit around her, but I tried to hold as much of her as I could.

"I will be out soon, then I can push you on your bike."

She was out of hospital in two weeks and a few weeks after that she was pushing me on the bike. The bigger I got the more my arms fit around my strong sister, and the age difference eventually faded as we both became adults. But even when homes separated us, our love and friendship never did.

That Jar-of-Marbles Car
By Kimberly Jamison

We had a good run in that car
that sounded like a jar of marbles
and let out more fumes
than a chain smoker.
We passed under the sails of windmills
that smelt like bread and jam.
We climbed to the top, clinging frantically
cowards, entwined hands.
We overheated during summer
and flooded our caravan.
We were stalked by seagulls
and swept through the air,
covered in mud
at that dodgy funfair.
We parked outside an abandoned chapel,
our home for the week.
It boasted a door that went to nowhere
and a shower that leaked.
We drove back tired,
stopping at the cheapest place,
ate breakfast sandwiches
half bacon, half grease.
Over the plastic table
you looked at me and swore
"I'll always keep
that jar-of-marbles car."

After Dover Beach
By Matthew Lewis Miller

There was something very strange about Matt –
a supercilious little man. Deliberate movements.
Abrupt speech. An intelligence that lurked behind
life-dulled eyes. He was a poet. I was intrigued.

We holed up in a small cottage by the sea.
Dover, right on the cliffs, all summer.
He would woo me with words, caressing me
with curiously constructed metaphors.

We'd lie in the garden in a daze
on grey Sundays. He'd gaze out across the sea,
marvel that just through that haze lay
a new language and culture. He was quick
to amazement, which I loved.

I lapped it up. Again, and again, and again.
Then the holidays ended and, like a bubble
that had flown too high, our insipid little
world died a death.

Matt indulged introspection
as he recommenced his work,
writing cultural criticisms;
the lurking danger of communism.
Opera nights.
Why this play or that
just wasn't quite right.
You get the idea.

Things strained onward for a spate,
the two of us having reached
a boiling, stifling stalemate.
Dangerously close to explosion.

To prevent a continued erosion
I suggested a change of scene.

From the garden overlooking the white cliffs,
I pressed him to recall how we'd dream
of sailing out over the restless sea.
Set sail for France, love, just you and me.

He agreed, grudgingly.
Tickets were booked.
But that romance I missed was still overlooked.
He'd brought his laptop, kept writing
his turgid shit.
Didn't spare my available tits
a solitary glance.
God, it's not as if
I didn't try.

On the way home, we were shut
in a cabin, alone.
He was leaning out of the window,
gazing down at the foaming sea,
"Thinking," he said, "just thinking."
Though not thinking of me.

Suddenly he jumped down,
back onto the bed. I made
to grab his shoulders, caress
his worried head. He leaned
across me to sift through his
luggage instead.
Finding his notebook with an
"Aha!" he jumped back onto
the window ledge.

"See!" he exclaimed, "How the sea meets the sky!"
"Shimmering and glistening, I wonder why
the sea doesn't speak, do you think maybe

it used to long ago?"

"I don't know love. I honestly don't know."

He sat sometime longer,
with a furrowed brow,
muttering about Plato
and working out how
the world would reprimand us,
if it could.
I imagined it rising up and
engulfing the useless bastard
in an almighty flood,
sent by God,
to rid the world
of bloody poets.

Hare Series 2 – Untitled #1
By Lydia Crump

Darkness
By Sanjana Parikh

Chapter One

Kate's eyes opened as she heard the scream. She sat up and listened, but all she could hear was the wind blowing. She got up and dusted off the sand from her pyjamas. Wait... sand? Her mind whirled as she looked around. It was dark. There was sand everywhere. Her eyes froze on something bright in the darkness. She approached it slowly, trying to work out what it was. Under the full moon light, she recognized it; an orange Barrel Cactus.

Kate realized she was in the Mojave Desert, a few miles from her house. Her heart started drumming. She didn't know how she had got here. Had she been sleepwalking? She'd never done it before, not even as a child. The hot June wind blew again, dirtying her blonde hair.

Then, Kate heard another scream. It sounded like someone was being tortured. She had to do something. She ran towards it. There was a girl in the distance, lying on the ground. A hooded figure was stood over her. Kate watched as he grabbed her by her t-shirt and lifted her in the air. The girl tried to move but the figure seemed to be too strong for her. The girl's eyes caught Kate's.

"Kate, please help me!" the girl shouted.

The hooded figure dropped her to the ground and turned around in an instant. Kate jumped behind a bush but it was too late. He had seen her. He marched over to her and dragged her towards the girl.

"No, no please, let me go. I promise I won't tell anyone." He grabbed her hair and threw her onto the ground. The girl tried to reach Kate's hand.

“Kate, please, help me,” she cried.

Kate closed her eyes and began to cry. She heard the girl cry out, and then everything went silent. She opened her eyes and looked at the girl. She was staring at Kate. Kate saw the knife protruding from the girl’s belly and screamed.

“Shut up,” the hooded figure said. “You’ve always been a cry baby. Always crying, always moaning, always complaining. I am so tired of you.” Kate looked up. She knew this man; his voice sounded familiar. She didn’t recognize him. It was like her mind had stopped working. He picked her up by t-shirt and threw her back down onto the ground. Kate fell on her back. She screamed and tried to get up but his leg was on top of her.

“I’m not letting you go this time.”

He leaned over to the girl and removed the knife from her belly. He raised his hand in the air and stabbed Kate in the stomach.

“No!” Kate shouted. She sat up. Her hand immediately reached for her belly but there was no knife or blood. She looked around her, but there was no sign of any bloody struggle.

“What’s wrong?” a voice asked. It was Kate’s Mother.

“What happened?”

“Bad dream,” Kate said.

TWO DAYS LATER

“What have we got?” Detective Edwards asked as he approached the crime scene.

"Allison McCall, age fifteen, local girl. Suspected cause of death is a single stab wound in the stomach. A tourist guide was out on a trek with a family. They saw the body and called it in," Detective Roy replied.

"What about the murder weapon?"

"We found a bloody knife lying a few feet away from the body. Rina has sent it to Forensics to check for fingerprints."

"The killer is a local," Edwards said.

"How do you know that?"

"It's almost impossible to find your way to town from here without proper guides. The killer knew what he was doing and where he was going."

Detective Edwards turned around to head back to the precinct. His eye caught something glistening on top of a dark green cactus.

"Roy!" he immediately called out to his colleague. Edwards wore his gloves and picked up the shiny blonde strand of hair.

"Do you think we can get a DNA sample out of it?" Roy asked.

"Definitely," Edwards smiled.

The Crown of Thorns
By T.R.J. Shelley

Chapter One: *The Crown of Thorns*

'In a world of thieves, the only final sin is stupidity.' – Hunter S. Thompson

Kurvik had never been fond of cities. Errental was no different – crowded, and stifling. Venders corralled the public, each seller trying to gain the largest crowd possible, whilst an unusual combination of stale sweat and the sweet honeyed aroma of Chinseng root hung potent in the air around the market stalls. A torrent of voices screeched and yelled in a hundred different tongues; Veltish, Yarhad, Engrokky – even some dialects that Kurvik had no knowledge of. It was a hive of haggling and poison, with each person struggling to gain a bargain.

Kurvik's stomach churned at the mindless chaos that thrived in the marketplace; a true example of the continent's diverse populace. In the distance the Wahvarraket towered high, its golden brown bricks shimmering quietly under the sun's gaze. The building was somewhat of an engineering marvel; Kurvik could only guess as to how long it had taken to build. Its sides were covered in murals and paintings, swirls of crimson and indigo, and every now and again, a splash of sapphire blue lapped at its corners, like waves breaking against the bow of a steadfast warship.

At its front, a magnificent archway cut apart the cold grey slabs that ran to the broad double doorway, that itself led to the city's council chambers. Before the entrance stood two guards, a move designed to keep out beggars and troublemakers alike. A lonely zephyr whipped through the marketplace. Having grown up in Karanev, Kurvik was accustomed to the mixed weather and watched intently as those from hotter climates recoiled in shock at the unexpected chill. Looking at the broad array of emotion in the crowds, he couldn't help but think of home, of the wet earth in autumn and the passing of the sun's favour that seemed to stay so fleetingly in the already brief summer months… but that was all in the past. Memories best left forgotten.

The doors opened and Kurivk's eyes locked onto the sudden movement. A procession of nobles came streaming out in a great march – a rag tag river of wealth. Soldiers seemed to materialize from surrounding alleyways, flanking their masters like impetuous guard dogs. Their bright ochre armour glistened as light bounced off of it. A scant few more seasoned veterans had chevrons emblazoned across their shoulders, imbued into the leather itself, a mark of their experience and bravery in battle. Their commander wore a dark crimson cape that flapped vehemently in the wind. Kurvik didn't know whether to be impressed or laugh at the ridiculousness of the entire charade.

"Make way for the assembly!" cried the commander.

Kurvik struggled to search his mind for the man's name, but it remained lost to him. An unimportant detail about an insignificant puppet. Many of the soldiers' faces were obscured by thick flowing cloth that weaved and slid its way around their heads. Only their eyes stood out, wide and worried at the potential for disaster that stood before them, so much so that a few clutched the hilts of their swords, ready to swipe at the crowds lest they get too close.

Kurvik felt his stomach twinge again, but he paid his anxiety no mind. There could be no mistakes. Not today. Not now. Too much planning had gone into this. There was no room for failure. His eyes scanned nearby rooftops for any sign of trouble, but there was nothing. His pawns were well hidden. Glancing back at the market place, everyone who held a small portion of sense scurried away, desperately wanting to give the soldiers a wide berth as they continued on towards the Polancis, Errental's speaking chamber, the place where all new laws were announced.

Despite the inherent danger, fools continued to press the soldiers' patience, skulking as near to the nobles as they dared, grovelling for assistance with sob stories that everyone had heard before. Amongst their ranks, Kurvik could make out amputees and victims of the Chak, a flesh eating disease, which had spread like wildfire in the passing weeks. The assembly had called it the work of the Gods, but Kurvik knew that they were wrong. There was only one God, and he was merciful.

No. This is the work of darker forces, he thought. *The kind that linger in shadows.*

No one knew how the disease started, but the end was always the same. Death. Slow, gory, and agonising. Once infected there was no cure. So far it had only affected the low classes of Errental, a thing twisted by the nobility to signify the Gods' favour for the current political system. Kurvik was certain it wouldn't last. It was only a matter of time.

Somewhere in the distance the shrill whistle of a Karpek sung wistfully in the air. *The signal.* Kurvik began to effortlessly manoeuvre his way forward, pushing through the crowd as if he was nought but a passing wind – unseen, unheard. His palms were damp with a light film of sweat, though he wasn't nervous. This was simply another job, no different from the last.

His target continued to waddle forward, surrounded by soldiers and other jumped up nobles, yet distinct by the purple toga he so regally wore about his overly chubby chest. His fingers were adorned with rich, gold rings and an assortment of other sparkly jewels. There were definitely rubies and emeralds there; no doubt they would fetch a high price on the black market, yet Kurvik had eyes for something else.

It was the crown. The crown of the high speaker of the assembly. A basic thing, made of old Heruk wood that had supposedly been blessed by Krineg himself, first of the Assarti's chosen. He was a God in all but name, and everyone this side of the Karabeli Sea bowed to the legend of his past deeds. He had been a hero, a unifier of men, and if the assembly's preaching was to be believed, the likes of which would never be seen again. That crown was worth more to Kurvik than anything in the world, not just in a practical sense, but spiritually as well. It had been taken from his people centuries ago. Wars had been waged over it, but ultimately they had ceded it to the people of Errental. A mistake that Kurvik intended to rectify. All he needed was a distraction.

And then there was one.

A bang echoed around the courtyard, making Kurvik's eardrums swell and pulse. The beggars nearest to him jolted upright, some moving with such sudden speed that they were but a blur. A dense powdered black smoke filled the air.

All around him Kurvik could hear people retch and recoil at the acrid stench that emitted from it. It always seemed to get to the back of your throat, and when that happened, bile followed. Though this wasn't the case for Kurvik. He'd grown up as a bit of an experimental alchemist, always creating concoctions by mixing together whatever ingredients he could get his hands on. It had given him a strange hardiness to chemicals that others simply didn't possess. Using it to his advantage, Kurvik pressed on amongst the commotion.

Everywhere people shouted and screamed, panicked and confused. He heard the commander shout, "Fall back! Protect the-" before his voice abruptly stopped, only to be filled by the sickly reassuring sound of vomit hitting the dusty earth below.

It was a well-timed disturbance, but it wouldn't last forever. Kurvik picked up his pace and sprinted at his target, however his visibility was poor and he very nearly ended up skewering himself on a roving spear.

Slowing his movement to something more manageable, Kurvik ducked and weaved his way to the Speaker. The man was on the floor, covered in a horrible filth, which was almost as colourful as a rainbow. Crouching low, Kurvik removed the crown from the man's greasy black hair and bowed in ceremonious thanks before removing himself from the situation, as the smoke began to dissipate and people started to regain their senses.

The path to freedom proved to be an arduous one, sending Kurvik down narrow alleyways and secret back passages. Somewhere far off in the distance the alarm rang out, reminding him that he didn't have long. In a matter of minutes the city guards would invoke Dabik, the right to treat everyone in the city as a suspect by shutting the gates to the vast world that lay beyond. They would turn their citizens into prisoners until the crown was returned to them, and the criminal punished for their crime. Kurvik, however, had no intention to be caught and by scrambling his way up the side of the city's shanty buildings, scaled his way towards the wall.

After a few minutes of climbing, only one last obstacle remained, but the wind had picked up – a strong gust that threatened to ruin everything.

Kurvik had to jump to the wall.

It was about twelve feet away to the other side. Down below was nothing but a sheer drop to certain death. A galling prospect. Kurvik's lungs were tender, a conspicuous burn having taken over his chest. Similarly his legs felt heavy, more like shackles than muscle. He wanted more than anything to rest and wait, but there was no time. It was now or never. Placing the crown in his left hand, Kurvik took a deep breath.

He let the air circulate around his body – waited for his fingers to tingle as his heart hammered in his temple, and then ran. It was a forced sprint, with every fibre of his being begging him to stop. Kurvik refused to listen to their refusal and pressed on. Putting every ounce of strength he had left into his thighs, he pushed off the ground and leaped forward. It was over in seconds, but seemed like he stayed in the air for minutes. In an instant he'd covered the gap and arrived at his destination.

His chest slammed into the wall and knocked the wind from his lungs. His right hand thrashed out wildly at the top and caught a hook of some kind, but Kurvik was weak and panicky. He looked down to find the crown still in his left hand and breathed a stifled sigh of relief. It didn't last long. In seconds a sharp pain sprang in his fingers, which screamed at him to let go. Kurvik tried to ignore it and haul himself up but his arms were insolent and unresponsive, oblivious to the severity of the situation. Kurvik began to flail and shuffle, trying to kick himself up the wall, but all it did was add more pressure to his fingers.

The pain was excruciating. He couldn't take anymore.

Kurvik yelped in frustration and watched in abject horror as his fingers slipped free from the hook and he fell back, tumbling down as wind rushed past his face and the cruel, unforgiving earth rose to embrace him.

The Writers' Mind

By Charlotte Porter

The Orla Scimitar Chronicles – Kiss This
By Andrew Henley

Orla's lips looked like she'd been chewing liquorice. Her raven-black lipstick had faded and dissolved on her lips in jail overnight. Her toned body was cloaked with tattoos beneath her itchy, orange jumpsuit. Maroon patches of moss and rust climbed the thick, metal jail bars, congregating around the heavy duty lock.

The Mexican guards had taken her cowboy hat. And her spurs. Leather jacket and jeans. Her deck of cards, her motorbike keys and her pearl grip pistol. A packet of kola kubes and her old brass lighter. And pictures. The worst thing they had taken were pictures.

Her hands were cuffed behind her back when they brought her in, the metal loops cutting away at her wrists as she resisted. The guards searched her pockets, pushing their hands up against her defenceless skin. Everything they took out was dropped loosely into an old cardboard box. One of the corners was crumpled and another had begun to split. The fattest guard stole her cowboy hat and placed it onto his oversized coconut shaped head. It was too small, balancing like fruit on Carmen Miranda.

They undid her handcuffs, pressed the orange jump suit into her arms and shoved her into a private room. Orla could have escaped then, but for the three Wasp SMGs pointing at her, wearing guards' fingers on their triggers.

Orla looked down at the black military print number stencilled on her prison uniform. 666. The guards didn't know what they were getting themselves into. She wore black leather boots with red skulls stitched into them and sharp silver spurs attached. Orla flicked her feet and the boots flew off to kick the door with a thud. She peeled off her thick leather jacket and tossed it on the floor. Underneath, she was naked.

The cobra tattoo on her shoulder hissed menacingly as a camera flashed through a makeshift peephole in the private door. Orla's fast fingers unzipped her black jeans with a penetrating bumblebee buzz. More camera flashes as she dropped them. All she had on were her red pair of panties with a blue trim and the Wonder Woman logo. Orla was petite enough that she could wear children's underwear. The tattoo on her right buttock was still visible. More camera flashes.

Orla stuck her middle finger up at the door and pointed to her tattoo. It was a pair of dark, pouted lips with the caption 'Kiss This'. The edges of the fresh tattoo still had red irritation marks around them.

She balled her clothes together and left the private peepholed room. One of the guards took the knotted ball of clothes and shoved it gracelessly into the cardboard box. It split a little more. A pair of cheap, and scuffed, black shoes were dropped in front of her. There was a wolf whistle as she bent over to put them on.

"Too big," she said.

"Smallest we got. Don't get many chiquitas."

Two guards grabbed her, one for each arm. They walked her through a long, damp hall with a rusty propane generator. At the end of it was a window box with a desk behind it. A crooked sign that read 'Front Office' hung over the window. The three Wasp SMGs followed her steps, although the guards holding them were too busy watching Orla's ass to notice if she tried anything. Best not to risk it.

“Name?” the old guard asked from behind the front office desk. He had a newspaper and didn’t look up. His nose was long, red and swollen, notched and ridged with capillaries that had risen to the surface for air. The skin on his neck was wrinkled and loose, like a turkey’s. Over his grey hair he wore a flat brown police cap with three forward facing points.

“Orla Scimitar,” she told him.

“Scimitar, Orla,” he repeated as he jotted it down.

He looked up at her and grinned wide, his grey eyebrows leaping up into his wrinkled forehead.

“Well, ho ho ho!” he laughed and his throat gobbled, “We don’t get many chiquitas through here!”

The Juan Arbeloa Correctional Facility was clearly starved of female inmates. Wolf whistles and catcalls surrounded her long walk to the dirty cell. One of the inmates grabbed Orla by her long, white hair and yanked her towards his jailbars as her guards simply watched. She kicked him sharply in the balls and shook herself free.

Orla’s cell was empty, except for two beds. She was glad to be alone. She ran her bare and bitten fingernails through her usually sleek hair, and instead felt knots and tangles. She knew the black streak that ran through it would be fading away too. Orla looked at her wrist as she fell asleep that night.

“Sorry, Ariel,” she whispered. Orla was not the type of girl to cry.

Her lips were liquoriced the next morning. Two guards dragged a sweating and potbellied man to her cell, and turned the key in the latch with a clunk, before pushing him inside. One of the guards was wearing her cowboy hat.

Orla rapped on the bars. "Shouldn't I be with a female inmate?"

The guard in her hat answered. "Sorry, Princess, you're the only chiquita here, and we're full up."

Her new cellmate suited this dark den of iniquitors; rapists, drug addicts and thieves. This was a place for petty thugs, and dumb ones at that. It was not a place for Orla, and she wouldn't be here long.

The prisoner cupped one of his flabby hands around her ass. "Hear y'all got a real purty tattoo, girlie," he said in a trailer park drawl.

"Take it off before I break it off." The words left Orla through bared canines and incisors.

He ignored her. "Something about you wantin' kissing? You in need of some lovin' girl? Hyuk, hyuk, hyuk."

Orla grabbed his wrist and twisted. There was a sound of bubble wrap popping, and a high-pitched scream. She slammed his head into the wall, leaving a cherry sunburst of blood as her cellmate slumped slowly in the corner.

"That's Solitary," the guard in her cowboy hat said.

He unlocked the cell and grabbed her by the arm in a rough grip. There were no guns pointing at her this time. There was nothing stopping her. Orla let the guard think he was in charge as she led him to Solitary.

As he turned the key in the door to Solitary, she leaned in close enough to smell the chilli on his breath and said, "You know, there are certain *benefits* of having a chiquita inmate…"

He flashed a smile of stained yellow teeth. "Oh yeah?"

As he leaned forward, Orla spun and kicked him in the back with her cheap prison shoes. As he tripped past her into the Solitary cell, she plucked her cowboy hat off his head. He lay still, and so she unlooped her keys from his belt before leaving. She pushed the door shut hard and locked him in.

Orla remained undetected as she made her way to the front office. The old guard was still sitting there, reading his newspaper. Orla jumped through the window and twisted his neck. It broke, his larynx crushed like a walnut. It did not make as satisfying a sound as her cellmate's wrist.

There was a pile of boxes on the shelf, all torn and frazzled in slightly different patterns. Orla looked through them, pulling them onto the floor until she found her own. As she stripped off her prison uniform, she felt the guard's dead eyes were still gawking at her naked body. She got dressed and put all of the stuff in the bottom of the box back into her pockets. The guards had eaten all of her kola kubes. They had taken the bullets out of her pistol, but left them in the box. She slotted them back into the chamber cylinders and tucked the gun into her pocket.

The brass lighter felt cold in Orla's hands as she took it from the box. A wry smile crept onto her liquorice lips. She looked under the guard's desk and found a half full bottle of vodka. She tore the 666 off her uniform and used it to cork the bottle.

Two guards walked past the office and saw her. Before they could grab their guns, Orla drew her pearl gripped pistol and shot them both in the forehead. The blood and wounds were like Indian jewels.

Orla jumped back through the window counter and stepped over the two bleeding bodies. She held the vodka bottle in her left hand and the lighter in her right. The key loop was her bracelet. She lit her prison number and it burned like the banner of a felled regime. Orla walked down the hall, opened the main door and threw the bottle back at the propane generator.

An explosion.

Orla walked away as the Juan Arbeloa Correctional Facility went up in flames. Her spurs stepped calmly along the dirt track, and Orla hitched down her black jeans and the cool breeze massaged her skin.

“Kiss This.”

Red Cruelty
By Elizabeth Cooper

It was that time of year when the ladybirds were out in full force, like small specks of dust floating in the air. They landed on Peg's window, looking ridiculous, with their little legs working so hard to shuffle their round bodies up the glass. Peg knelt on his bed, elbows on the windowsill. He leant out and placed his stubby finger for the ladybird to crawl up. It played dead, then, it looked for a new way round. Peg kept forcing the ladybird to climb onto his hand until his patience wore thin. He pinched it between two fingers. Its little legs flailed as its feet were pulled from the glass.

"What are you complaining about? You could've flown away." Peg smirked.

He brought it over to his desk, turning on the lamp. He pulled a pair of tweezers from a drawer.

"How do you fly anyhow?"

Peg placed the insect's feet into a drop of glue and put it on a piece of paper. It wriggled, trying to scuttle away. It opened its red spotted wings and flapped them, helpless. Peg picked at the casing with his tweezers. He bent one at the joint – it snapped off.

"Here are your wings."

He lifted the other half of the casing and broke that off too. The ladybird squirmed, but it couldn't move. Its wings, iridescent in the lamplight, fluttered weakly. With the help of the cold metal points, he grabbed both sets and ripped them off, then laid them in size order, beside the red casing.

"Peg! Come down. Dinner's ready," called a voice from the hall.

He put the tweezers down, leaving the ladybird to die.

The insect lay in the puddle of glue, wingless.

Rain Sparkled Origami
By Andrew Henley

Under the dark velvet skyline, raindrops fell on an emerald forest gathered at the edge of Hokkaido. Every leaf clung to the sparkling liquid that fell from the sky; only nature recognized the true power of its magic. Later, these trees were cut down and pulped.

Grandma Chen bought a ream of paper from her local market. The sheets were a rainbow of colours, which sparkled subtly under the dull sun. Grandma Chen used the first sheet, a marshmallow pink colour, to write a letter to her granddaughter, Xiao Chen, who lived in London. She then put the letter and the rest of the unused ream of coloured paper into box and took the box to the post office.

A week later, Xiao Chen received a package. She opened it and read the letter. Grandma Chen is proud of her, and hopes she does well with her exams. Xiao is due to take her A-Levels the following month, and is set to pass with top marks. But tonight is not supposed to be about studying.

Tonight is Xiao Chen's prom night, and as she read her grandma's letter she is sitting on her bed in a long, elegant, silver evening dress. It swayed as if it were made of mercury, flowing loose and smooth.

Her shoes are sharp-toed, pink stilettos. Xiao isn't sure if they match the dress, but she likes them enough to not care. There's not much she can do with her black, boyish, face-framing bob, but it has been well brushed, and is always straight. Her makeup was as lightly applied as she could manage.

Xiao Chen is not going to the prom.

No one would take Xiao. She has high Asian cheekbones, but the kids at school can only see her yellow tinged skin. They see slits for eyes, magnified by black, thick-rimmed glasses, when in reality Xiao has the big blue orbs of a manga comic character. She is a ricepicker and a brainiac, not to be talked to or trusted.

She read through her grandma's letter once more. It told her that the stack of papers was for her origami, for her to continue practising and keep in touch with her Japanese heritage. Everyone else would be out dancing and kissing and clumsily touching each other's bodies in dark corners. Xiao could almost hear the electric clicks of high heels on the dance floor, the sound of nova explosions; the death of stars.

While everyone made friends and lived their lives, Xiao Chen folded paper. She turned in corners and bent edges upwards until she made a cobalt blue cat. It was impressive, but that just made it sadder. As Xiao turned and looked out of the window with longing eyes, the sparkle seeped through the paper. Xiao heard a mewling purr, and felt something furry rubbing against her leg. She looked down and saw a cobalt cat. It jumped on her lap and looked at her with a watery glimmer in her irises. Xiao stroked her new kitten as it continued to purr, then it curled up and fell asleep.

Xiao picked up another sheet of her grandma's paper, ruby red this time, and folded with concentration. She made a dragon. She stared at it for ten seconds and her disappointment grew. It was still paper. Her eyes wandered around the room, feeling foolish. When she looked back at where the origami dragon was, it had disappeared. There was a low grunting behind her, and an enormous red dragon was standing next to her. A grin crept across its wispy lips as it exuded thick grey smoke from its cavernous nostrils.

Xiao stretched out her arm to reach for a bookshelf to her left. Moving carefully, so as not to disturb her cat, she grabbed her yearbook. She wouldn't even have one if her family back in Japan hadn't asked her to get one. On the day they were handed out, Xiao was grateful she had been able to hide hers in her satchel before anyone had written anything mean on it. She held it up to the dragon, who obediently and excitedly blew a dagger of flames that engulfed the yearbook whole.

Next, Xiao created four paper canaries of sunny yellow. She lined them up in a row. They were inanimate, so she closed her eyes. When she opened them again, they were flying around her head as if she had been bonked with a hammer in a cartoon.

With the cat asleep on her lap and the canaries swooping around the dragon, Xiao folded her grandma's marshmallow pink letter into the shape of her favourite animal. She snapped her eyes shut, and as they popped open, a pink panda stood in front of her. He offered out his paw and held Xiao Chen's hand. She slid the cat off her knee and it twitched sleepily. In her silver prom dress, Xiao stood hand in hand with the panda. He put his other paw on her hip and they danced around the room. Outside, the rain sparkled against her window.

The Words
By Eliza Gradwohl

Her tear stained the paper just like the ink did. She sniffled slightly trying to keep it in. She was determined not to cry in the school library. It was so quiet that if she were to release her sobs all the attention would be on her in a second, yet she knew she would find no help here. She wasn't going to break – not in front of all of her peers, not in the hell hole she was obliged to go to every day for six hours, not for such a stupid reason. She stared down at the paper and then up again, looking straight at the pack of teenage boys who had placed it on her desk. They thought they were so cool because they could bring someone else crashing to the ground and use that person's destruction to build themselves higher. They were laughing, clutching their stomachs at the look on her face, the look of pure hurt. Whoever said the rhyme *sticks and stones may break my bones but words will never hurt me* had **lied**. She would much rather have all 206 bones broken than have to read the words on the ripped piece of blue and white lined paper. She crumpled it up, trying to crush the words, looking for some form of satisfaction, but receiving none. Her eyes were burning, and she tried to gulp down the knot forming in her throat. She quickly stood up and grabbed her brown messenger bag, slinging it over her shoulder before running to the grimy school bathroom. The paint was peeling off the walls and it smelled strongly of a perfume that no one would ever find pleasant. There were five metal stalls in a row, each getting more disgusting as you moved closer to the one on the end. She closed herself into the last one, letting the hot tears spill slowly from her eyes and travel down her heart shaped face. She gasped for air and used her sleeve to blot at her eyes in the hope of seeing again. That was a big mistake.

When her vision cleared up a bit, her eyes caught her name on the side of the stall. She bent down, inspecting the writing more thoroughly. It was a conversation. About her. As she read through the black scribbles, rivers started forming. The pain she felt was worse than anything she could imagine. Worse than the jagged cuts she created on her skin every night. Worse than being thrown into metal lockers. Worse than finding out the boy you loved had no feelings for you and loved your best friend instead. She would gladly have taken any of those actions compared to having to read the wrinkled piece of paper, or the harsh black words on the side of the stall. She grabbed a wad of toilet paper and blotted at her eyes, desperate for a break. Hoisting her bag back onto her shoulder, she decided to make a break for her locker. She quickly unlocked it, but not before a group of girls passed her, throwing wads of paper at her and calling her names. Tears started streaming uncontrollably down her face and she felt something inside her break even more. She grabbed her jacket and thrust her arms into it, hoisting her bag onto her shoulder before taking off. She passed Mrs Mayer's room and saw her favourite teacher's face contort with fear and worry as she saw her walking quickly through the halls. She heard Mrs Mayer call after her but she paid no attention, speeding up her pace instead. She made a mad dash for the doors, passing the assistant principal as she did, and heard him request for her to stop. She only increased her speed, desperate to leave, bursting through the main doors. She didn't stop running until she was off of school grounds. She stopped to catch her breath and figure out where she was going. Home was crossed off her list immediately. She didn't want to deal with her older brothers now – they didn't understand. They never understood. The library would normally be her next choice but it was too predictable. If she went there she would probably get caught. So, she decided to go to the park.

All she felt was pain. The pain started at her core and slowly travelled until it covered every bone, every muscle, and every cell of her being. Her feet carried her on the familiar path to the park, but she wasn't participating in reality. The words and names she had been called swam around in her brain, cutting her sharper and deeper than her razor with every memory. Hot tears continued to roll down her cheeks as memories came flooding through like a dam that had burst from constant pressure. She wiped furiously at her face but it did no good. All too soon her sneaker clad feet hit the dank woodchips, signalling she had reached her destination. She followed a small path until she reached the swing set and sat down on the one in the corner, throwing her bag down next to her. She sat there and cried, silent, slowly rocking back and forth.

She was so oblivious to the world that she didn't notice a group of teenage boys walking into the park and onto the basketball court. She was too hysterical to recognize them as the boys from the table, the ones who had given her that tiny wrinkled piece of paper. But they noticed her immediately. They strode over to her, smirks planted on their faces, and swooped in like eagles before she even had time to whisper help. She wished they would hit her, kick her, beat her senseless. That would have been less painful, but their soft jagged tongues cut her down swiftly. They were expert loggers and they wasted no time in trying to get her to fall down. It wasn't hard either. By now, she believed every single word they said. There was no one to tell her that they were wrong, in fact, it was just the opposite. Everyone agreed with them, everyone told her the same things, over and over again. Eventually, the group of trying-to-be-cooler-than-they-will-actually-ever-be high school students grew tired and went to go play their game of basketball. She fell from the swing, collapsing onto the ground, her head dropping onto her knees for support. She heard her phone go off and grabbed it, reading the text message in her hand.

> From: Danny- *Why aren't you in school? Where are you?*

She didn't respond. A second later, her phone went off again.

From: Davey- *We are worried sis. Where are you?*

She hesitated. Then, she wrote:

To: Davey & Danny- *At the park. Coming home x*

Instantly, her phone buzzed again.

From: Danny- *Screw that. Coming to get you. Stay put. You're in trouble.*

She grabbed her bag and started walking fast, regretting she had responded in the first place. She loved her older brothers but they could be a bit intense. She understood why, partially. It wasn't easy, having to raise your sixteen year old sister a year after you graduated from college. Her older brothers were twins, Davey being the younger of the two. Danny was always the mature one, but he used to be more fun. Then, their parents got into the car accident and died. Danny and Davey got custody of their little sister and things never returned to normal. She stopped expecting them to either. Davey, who used to be the cool, chill one that she could share everything with and never be judged, grew farther away from her, never having the time to listen to anything she had to say. Danny turned into a hard ass that was stricter than her parents ever were, often blaming her for anything that went wrong. She never tried hard enough, never co-operated, spent too much money, always acted out, could never do what she was told, and made life increasingly harder in every way. She felt more like a nuisance than anything, like an unwanted pet. They never wanted her around, she felt, but always wanted her home so she couldn't create any drama or trouble. When she was home she was alone, and if she tried to hang out with them she was always asked why she wasn't doing something productive. Sometimes, they would still fall back into their old natures, but it wasn't natural, and they would change again faster than a chameleon. She just wanted her old brothers back.

She let the old memories of them playing together consume her as she started wandering, not knowing where she was going but trying to put enough space as possible between her and the park. She looked around for a familiar golden car, content when she didn't see one. She didn't want to face the brothers that would be disappointed in her, the brothers that would punish her without asking questions or letting her explain, the brothers that upset her. She wanted the brothers that would listen to her, talk to her, and try to help her. She wanted the brothers that made her feel safe, the brothers who would do anything to see her smile, and the brothers who cared about her and loved her. After a while, she heard her phone go off again and she picked it up to read it.

From: **Danny-** *Where the hell are you?! Stop playing games!!*

She pocketed her phone, not bothering to respond. She didn't want to be found. She didn't want to explain. They never wanted to hear her out anyways. She would just get punished for leaving school and acting out. She walked past stores on the main street, absorbed in her own thoughts. The damaging words came surfacing again, but she had no tears left. She stopped and turned to face a window where she could see her reflection. Her eyes were bloodshot and her nose was red. Her cheeks were streaked and her hair was a mess from her hands constantly running through and pulling at it. Her eyes wandered down to her stomach and thighs, to her overall height and figure. They were right and she knew it. All the words they said, all the messages they wrote, they were one hundred percent true. She turned to the main road with a burning pain in her heart.

All she wanted was for the pain to go away. She only wanted to be free of the entrapping words and the immobilizing hurt that followed. She wanted her parents back, her self-esteem back, her friends back. She wanted the happiness back. She didn't think about it, she didn't even hesitate. She saw the truck coming from down the road and quickly pulled out her phone. She typed in a new message:

To: **Davey & Danny-** *I love you x*

She hit the send button, pocketed her phone, and took a deep breath. She slid her bag up higher on her shoulder and stepped closer to the road. No one noticed. No one cared. No one appeared to be the voice of reason or to create doubt in her mind. The truck continued to roll closer. Her phone dinged once, and then again a second later. She took another deep breath and another step. She closed her eyes. She heard the squeal of tires and a horn honking. Suddenly, she felt like she was flying. She felt pins and needles race from one side of her body through her to the other. Then she hit the ground. For a brief moment, she was in more pain than she had ever felt in her entire life. It was as if all of her pain from the inside had escaped and was now on her outside. Then, the world went black and she felt herself flying once more.

The words stopped haunting her. The voices and faces that had said all those harsh words stopped swimming around her head. She wasn't aware of anything other than that. She heard familiar voices, distant but frantic, somewhere above her, but darkness was swallowing her up. She didn't fight it; she accepted it like an old friend. It gave her a pleasant numbness and a relaxing quiet. She knew that the words couldn't touch her here. She slowly sank into the numbness as the voices became less coherent, more of a buzz, fading as if someone was turning the volume down. She sank lower and lower until she was aware of nothing but the calming darkness. And that is where she found her peace.

***

The people on the street stopped to stare. One moment the pretty, petite girl was standing on the sidewalk texting, the next she was in the middle of the street in front of an oncoming truck. The truck tried to stop, the driver slamming on the brakes and turning, but it still hit her. She was sent flying in the air and landed hard on the concrete of the road. There was a haunting crack that rang clear throughout the still air and shocked crowd, and some of her limbs stuck out at odd, unnatural angles. A golden car, which was behind the truck, pulled over, and two identical young men got out of it, running toward the scene. They checked on the truck driver first, who just seemed shocked, and then rushed to the figure. Once they saw the limp girl, they started screaming, calling out a name, one even started crying. People began gathering around her, pushing to the front to see the boys calling her name with urgency, shaking her, but stopping after realizing how limp her body was. They looked shockingly like the girl, sharing the same brown hair and the same skin tone, a nice golden white colour. The twins glanced around, seeing many people on the phone with the emergency dispatcher, telling them it would be another ten minutes until help arrived. They just looked back down, continuing to call out her name, desperately waiting for a reaction that would never come.

Hare Series 2 – Untitled #2
By Lydia Crump

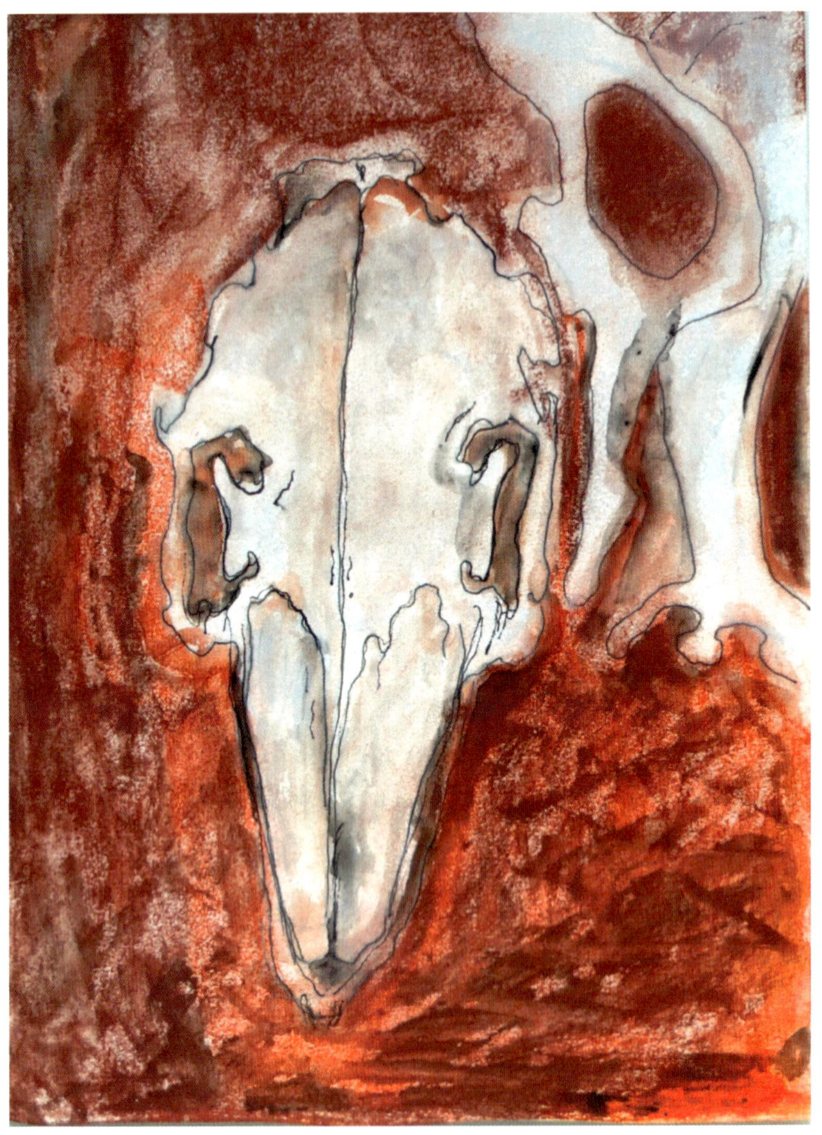

Education, Education, Education

By Matthew Lewis Miller

Take this bubbling vat,
add fish heads
and allow to simmer.

Pour into polystyrene cups,
sold at friendly faced stalls
for reasonable prices,
and sip slowly throughout your life.

You'll be glad of the sustenance
and will have at least one photo
to show your children.

Enjoy the privilege.
People elsewhere would die
to dip their tongue
into this concoction.

After Work in Central London
By Liam Powell

Robert Maloney had always seen Central London as an idyllic location. In his opinion, the vibrancy of the place was second to nowhere else in the world. There was always something happening, always a large crowd, always a great atmosphere. Robert had always loved living and working there, and he doubted that would change anytime soon.

Tonight, however, he was not enjoying the setting, or indeed anything. His wife, Katie, had long suspected him of cheating. Robert had been unaware of this until last week, suspecting nothing out of the ordinary until she had stormed in one night. Apparently she had proof.

Robert had been furious. He had been brought up well by his parents, he said, and infidelity was not an option. He had demanded that she show him this proof, that she provide the name of her source. Katie had refused, on the idea that Robert would go and see the person in question, perhaps attack them. She had even suggested he would bribe them.

"You think I would *bribe* this guy?" Robert had said the words quietly, barely more than a whisper, though he knew that there was a rage boiling inside.

"I know you would."

"FUCK YOU!" Robert had raised his fists, so angry with his wife that for a split second the idea of hitting her had crossed his mind. He had managed to control it and instead lashed out at the wall, leaving a mark that served as a constant reminder of the moment.

"That's not really helping your case, Robert." Katie had said it in such an assured manner that it had scared him. Clearly there was absolute certainty in her mind that he had been seeing another woman. She had gone on to say that she believed the affair had been going on for several months.

"And you believed that?" Robert had asked her.

"Yes, I do!"

"Then I don't know why I'm even bothering!" he said, fuming.

"Then don't," Katie had replied.

That night Katie had packed a bag and told him she was staying with her sister. Robert had rung over and over again, but no answer had come. Finally, after five days of this, Katie had relented. She was still angry, but was prepared to meet him for dinner. A posh restaurant just off Leicester Square, an Italian place, Robert had forgotten the name.

As he got ready for the meal, he drank a beer, not capable of relaxing without one. His marriage was on the line, potentially over, after doing nothing wrong. He insisted upon his innocence all along, not accepting the accusations for a split second. Katie was equally convinced. He had been meeting another woman for months; numerous people had confirmed the same name to her.

And although Robert consistently protested his innocence, Katie was not interested in alternative stories. He knew she was stubborn, it was one of the things he loved about her, but to refuse to even listen to him wasn't fair, he felt. And as the days went by with her unfaltering belief that it was true, he began to fear if he would ever get her to believe him.

Downing the remainder of his beer, he threw the empty bottle towards the bin and watched as it bounced back off the lip and smashed on the floor.

"Brilliant," he said to himself. "Just the start I need." He searched the cupboards for a dustpan and brush, cursing that he couldn't find it. Katie had always dealt with that stuff, and with a sudden pang he stopped.

He had not considered everything that he would miss if Katie did not return home, like the little things that she did quietly every day, things that he had not even noticed. The beautiful Canary Wharf apartment was spotless – though at this moment it had several pizza boxes on the coffee table – and, as Robert looked around it, he realized that it was not that way because of him.

It was Katie that did the cleaning, Katie that did the cooking, Katie that made this place look perfect every day. How would he be able to cope without her doing all of that? Robert had never looked after himself before. He had moved out of home, into a full-catered halls at university, where he had met Katie, and been living with her ever since.

He ran his fingers through his thick, dark hair and sighed. He knew Katie had quietly been a rock for him, staying at home while he had gone to work and earned for them both. He had never really appreciated how tidy she had kept the place.

Not bearing to look at the constant reminders of Katie's input to the living room – even the cream and brown decoration was her doing – Robert walked into the bedroom, leaving the shards of glass by the bin. He experienced another sharp pang as he saw the picture of himself and Katie on his bedside table. It had been taken on their wedding day; the single greatest moment of his life. Where had it all gone wrong?

Trying to ignore the rising sense of panic, he picked up his suit jacket and put it on carefully. He had specifically chose the grey pinstriped one, knowing that it was Katie's favourite. Give yourself every chance, he had told himself, when deciding on what to wear. He checked his watch and felt another stab of pain – Katie had brought it for him – before taking in the time of 7.30. It was time to go and see if he was to remain married, and as he locked the door to his apartment, he was getting a much clearer idea of what the alternative would be like.

***

The restaurant was busy. Not the worst thing in the world, he thought, as the last thing he wanted was to be overheard. He felt a crowded setting would help avoid that. His worst fear was seeing someone he knew. Nearly all of his work colleagues lived in London and regularly dined in the area, Robert didn't think he would be able to cope with bumping into one of them. None knew of the delicate problems he was experiencing at home.

He had purposefully arrived fifteen minutes early, as he knew that Katie would be on time, and being late was the last thing he needed. That kind of thing irritated her at the best of times.

After a few moments, a waiter approached. Robert ordered another beer, his nerves getting worse. He could feel the sweat running down his back. As the waiter returned, Robert noticed a stunning brunette approach the door. She was tall and slim, with her hair straightened to shoulder length, wearing a black dress that complimented her perfectly, and as his wife walked in Robert did not divert his gaze. He knew that Katie would make an effort for tonight, but he had not expected this.

As she took her seat opposite him, Robert began once more to consider life without her, and swallowed at the realization that he would struggle to find another woman this attractive.

Katie looked calm, but serious. Her stunning appearance did not hide the anger that Robert could see was clearly still inside her, and as she placed her coat over the back of her chair, she threw him a look. Annoyed with himself, Robert realized too late that he should have stood and taken her coat off for her.

"Can I get you drink?" he asked.

"White wine spritzer."

Robert smiled at her. Some things never changed. His smile faltered as she returned it with a stern look, as if amazed that he had the audacity to so much as smile. He called the waiter over and relayed the order, requesting menus at the same time.

“Order whatever you like,” he told her. “I’m paying.”

“I would imagine so,” she said. “Seeing as you cheated on me.”

“I did not.” Robert tried to keep calm. Causing a scene was hardly likely to help the matter. But sudden accusations were making that a far more difficult task. “I thought we were going to discuss this?”

“We are,” replied Katie, “but don’t think I’m going to make it easy for you.”

“That’s hardly fair.”

“It’s hardly fair that you’ve been sleeping with another woman for six months.”

“I have not.”

“Liar.”

Robert had hoped Katie would have calmed down over the last week, seen the reasoning behind him being allowed the chance to at least defend himself. He had even been foolish enough to believe that her sister would have persuaded her that her husband might just have stuck to the vows he had made on their wedding day, not yet three years previously. Apparently not.

Trying to take the heat off for a few moments, Robert looked around the restaurant. It was a decent sized place, with a high class of clientele as every man in the vicinity was dressed in a suit. The atmosphere was one of elegance, tranquillity, as the diners held their own conversations. Robert envied them.

Surrounded by that, here he was, threating over whether his marriage would even make it until the desserts. The waiter returned with Katie's drink and placed two menus on the table.

Robert murmured a brief thanks to the waiter and looked back at Katie, who was watching him closely. She had never been an emotional character, but Robert could see the sadness in her eyes. Though they were not tear-filled, he knew that this was hurting her deep down. The type of character she was, Robert knew she would not let it show; would not let him see weakness when she was so convinced that he had done wrong.

"I love you, Katie," he whispered, as much through desperation as anything. He grabbed her hands, but instantly she pulled them out of his grip. "How can you not believe I don't love you?"

"I never said you didn't," said Katie, "but there's no doubt in my mind that you cheated on me."

"I swear, Katie. I swear to God I never did, I never could. I love you too much. I could never hurt you like that."

"Even if you didn't," Katie said slowly, "I won't ever believe you."

"You have to believe me," said Robert, "I never cheated."

"You can't ever prove that." Katie still looked composed, though Robert knew that her own words were causing her pain. He looked into her blue eyes, and could see the emotion inside of her, determined to be kept at bay. He was shaking now, an ever-increasing fear that he was about to lose the only woman he had ever loved. A fear that she was not going to believe what he desperately needed her to.

"But you don't want it to end, do you?" He was scared of what the answer would be, but he needed it announced. He needed to know what the situation was. He was desperate for Katie to believe him, to come and see the reason that he would not cheat on her, that he loved her too much to do such a thing.

But he would not beg. It was not in his principles to beg, not his nature to apologize for a thing he did not do. He had done nothing wrong, and would not behave as though he had. He had asked her repeatedly to believe him, and he had not hidden how desperate he was that she did, but if she would not relent then nor would he.

"You won't admit it?" said Katie, after a few moments of thought.

"I have nothing to admit. I love you more than anything, but I will not say sorry for something I never did."

"Then yes. I do want this marriage to end. You say you never cheated, and I am certain that you did. There will always be doubt. It's for the best."

Katie suddenly stood up, grabbed her handbag and made to leave the restaurant.

"You're making a mistake, Katie." Robert was torn – a contest between the desire for them resolve this, and his principles not allowing him to accept blame for anything he had not done. Katie stopped and looked back at him.

"There will always be doubt," she repeated. "I'm sorry, Robert."

And without a backwards glance, Katie walked out of the restaurant, leaving a disbelieving Robert sat at the table. As he watched her walk past the window, he breathed deeply, trying not to allow any of his emotion out.

"I take it you won't be ordering, sir?" Robert hadn't noticed the waiter return.

“I’m afraid not, sorry.”

A few moments later, as Robert stood outside the restaurant, he considered his options. Home was the last place he wanted to go right now, and he knew speaking to anyone about what had just happened would result in him crying, something he refused to let people see. Opting for a few more drinks, he walked towards the row of pubs in the distance.

As he passed a crowded bus stop he heard snippets of irrelevant conversation, until a particular piece made him pause.

“…So how do you feel?”

“Well, I’ve been with him since I was 19. It wasn’t going to be easy.”

“Did he admit to cheating?”

“No. To be honest, I doubt he did…”

Robert continued walking, having heard enough. If anything, what he had just heard had helped. Seeing his wife, with what he presumed was her new lover, accidentally reveal the whole thing was, in fact, a way for her to get out of the marriage. It was not easy, but as he headed for the pub, he knew one thing. He wasn’t going to be ringing her again.

Home
By Kimberly Jamison

Maybe it is in the stench of the rubbish tip that overlooks the town
Or the scratch of the coarse nylon bus seat covers.
Maybe it is in the glare of the black sharpie graffiti
Or the tired eyes of the barely legal mothers.

Maybe it is in the flashing glass of last night's riot
Or the rows of boarded up shop fronts.
Maybe it is in the grey sludge river
Or the shank discarded on the floor for being too blunt.

Maybe it is in the way we walk, head down, keep to yourself
Or the extra bolts, broken, on the elderly lady's door.
Maybe it is in the way the streets are emptied for safety
Or the adamant cries of "we ain't poor!"

Maybe it is in the meat van that bleeds with so-called 'bargains'
Or the bus driver who requires your change to be exact.
Maybe it is in the way the buskers can tell if you're a copper or paper person
Or the big issue sellers awkward eye-contact.

Maybe it is in the faults we see perfection
Or the stagnation that makes us roam.
Maybe it is in the way we can't choose our family
Or the place we finally call our home.

Drive
By Andrew Henley

Hitchhiking cacti
beg for
a ride. Tom Collins
shadows stretch
back to civilization.

The burnt out sun
of a cigarette sets
between the thick valley of two dirty fingernails,
snakes of smoke along a
desert dirt track.

Stop sign red paintjob,
scratched and scuffed
by whiskey steering.
One hand drums to
dashboard blues.

Carrion birds in the bleeding sky
watch hot erosion of
a hipflask swig.
The drumming stops.
A horn in the oncoming lane.

Untitled (1)
By Uta Feinstein

Babysitting
By Nicola Monaghan

It wasn't long after dinner and I'd watered the plants like my mum'd nagged at me about, and then Issie started choking. She was coughing and spluttering and holding onto her throat, and to be honest with you I thought she was messing about. She could be an irritating little shit sometimes. Always falling on herself and tripping up and then telling me I'd done it so that I'd be like, if I'd done it you wouldn't have to tell me all those details, would you, cause I'd know them? I was in the front room doing my nails when she ran through clutching her throat. I didn't take it seriously at all, but it was weird because I thought, that'd be just like our Issie, to choke to death while I was babysitting, just to get me done for it.

The thing is, her lips went blue and there was all this spit coming out her nose and I kept asking her and asking her what was wrong. She didn't answer and I thought she was just being awkward, and then I looked into her eyes and realized she couldn't talk. That was when I got scared. I tried to remember what my mum'd said about choking. She'd given me this lecture one time but I wasn't really listening because she went on about stuff a lot. I had to switch off or it'd have driven me mental. I went and slapped Issie on the back, cos I'd seen someone do that on the telly, but it didn't seem to be working and I thought then that she was going to die and it'd be all my fault.

I looked up 'choking' up on my iPhone, but it was loading really slow and all I could think was that Issie might die and it'd all be because we lived in a 'signal blackspot' like my dad kept telling me when I moaned 'cause I couldn't get on Facebook. The only thing I could think was to turn her upside down. I don't know what made me think of that but some logic inside me said that I might be able to make the sweet fall all the way out if I held her upside down and shook her. So I did.

I grabbed Issie tight round the waist and flipped her over. She was all kicking and wiggling and didn't like it one bit, but I was trying to save her life and thought she could put up with it for a minute. I held her right upside down and shook her as hard as a I dared and, on the second go, this tiny metal thing flew out her mouth and across the room, hitting the opposite wall then slipping to the floor and leaving a trail on the wallpaper. She started crying then and I knew she'd got her lungs back because she was making that wailing noise she was so bloody good at. I turned her back the right way up and put her down on the floor. She curled up in a ball and wouldn't look at me, as if I'd been the one who'd made her put some metal thing in her mouth instead of saving her when she was choking.

There was something shiny and slimy on the floor next to Issie. I picked up this gross object and realized it was my heart pendant with my birthstone in it. My Uncle Steve had got it me for my birthday and it was a lovely present cos I knew he'd thought hard about it, and Uncle Steve isn't usually good at buying presents. It was covered in spittle and phlegm and smelled of my sister's insides. I picked it up using the ends of my fingers, touching as little of it as I could, and then I wiped it on the sofa.

I was mad that Issie'd been in my room and took my stuff but I thought I couldn't say so, given that she'd nearly died and all that. She'd stopped crying but her face was still red and she was sucking her thumb and it made me feel sorry for her. I knew she liked to play Candy Crush on my phone, even though she didn't really know what she was doing. She liked the music, and the pictures of sweets. I loaded the game and passed her the phone.

"Don't get any snot on it," I said.

Issie looked up at me blankly. She smiled down at the phone and started to play and it was like she'd forgot all about nearly dying. I hoped so, because I reckoned I'd still get done if she told mum, even though I'd saved her life and they should be throwing garlands of flowers round my feet and buying me iPads to thank me. Parents are thick sometimes.

For some reason, I wanted to ask Issie if she was okay. But she was gone, hypnotised by the colours and music, and wouldn't have heard a word I said anyway.

I put my birthstone pendant on. It still smelled a bit like Issie but I didn't mind.

Parental Syndrome
By Sean Keenan

Her hunger is sated
…For now.
In around four hours she will awaken.
Bawling an ear piercing Banshee scream,
That makes you beg for the amity of sleep.

Her eyes stalk you like a hunter,
They are whimsical to your own, alluring.
She clings for you with such force,
Any attempts to appease her she refuses.

She lures you in with a sweet, tender smile,
As you lean closer she reaches out for you.
Her chubby fingers become talons,
As she claws for your eyes.

But you bring yourself to a smile,
As you watch her tranquil sleep,
One day, she'll tell you she loves you.
And will make all the timeless nights worth it.

Your peace blankets close tightly
Over your bloodshot, uninhabited eyes
Suddenly from the other room, you hear a shuffle.
Followed by a soft familiar cry

Dear god she has awakened.

Hills

By Eleanor Hemsley

I woke up and straight away I could feel the difference. There was something stopping my stomach from lying flat and evenly on the bed, something stopping me from being able to breathe as easily as usual.

I managed to roll myself over and felt something heavy on my chest. I lifted my head slightly to look down my body, only I didn't see it. Instead there were two, small hills, yet they were big enough to block the view of my feet that poked up somewhere behind them.

I couldn't help but smile. Finally, I thought, finally. I lifted my disproportionately small hands to the hills and rested them there. My nails lit up the skin and I marvelled at the colourful raindrops they made. I should repaint them, I thought, shaking my head at the chipped varnish that revealed me as an amateur. My sister always said it took months of practise to get it perfect.

I stood up, then almost fell over, forgetting to account for the new addition to my chest. After regaining balance I tottered over to the door and opened it, stretching my hobbit toes as I did so.

The house was surprisingly quiet for a Thursday morning. I walked into the bathroom, pulled down my pants and sat on the toilet, thinking of which dress I would buy next. I sighed.

"Seven down, only two more to go," I whispered, as I shook my penis dry.

Tassel Tree
By Kaya Gromocki

Taken in Alderly Edge, Cheshire

Self-Portrait As A Moth

By Matthew Lewis Miller

Sensing the close threat of compulsion,
he lives his life as a matter of convenience.
Blue lightshades bob before him
and emit occasional sparks
which entice him –
flapping and battering into various crates of cargo,
he flits near enough to feel the heat
of their electric hum
before veering away to some other windowsill
to enjoy the vast blinding comfort
of fresh white-wash paint.

I Think This Is the Day I Turn Veggie

By Kimberly Jamison

I think this is the day I turn veggie,
my fish fingers look like
they're breathing as they cook.

I try to make amends
by saving them from the oven
but now they're stuck to the tray
and my attempts at rescue
leave them crippled and mangled.

I should just eat them,
so I grab a few slices of white
and tuck them into their death bread.
But they can't get to sleep,
I think this is the day I turn veggie.

Two Acquaintances
By Alexandrea Cook

X : How long have we known each other?

Y : Since we first met I suppose.

X : What?

Y : We have known each other since we first met.

X : Sometimes I really hate talking to you.

Y : Only sometimes?

X : Isn’t that enough?

Y : Not really, I’ve hated talking to you for a while now.

X : Since when?

Y : Since we first met.

My Nut-jobs.
By Cara Da Silva

Deranged those strange lumps,
Tearing theological verses to my throat,
Throwing rules and governing our woeful,
Penniless house with jail bars and alarms,
Unhealthy, god-fearing asylum-
Mrs Bossy and Mr Fat,
Prodding around waiting for our egg brains to crack,
Oppress us more when we cry, with your unsound words,
Sway punishment here and there.
Spiritual guidance, ha! Who's there?
Ignorance and neglect to your children,
That's not honest or fair,
Nevertheless, scowling eyes, a tearful physical battle,
Abnormal upbringing,

They don't care.

If Love was the Fluff between Your Toes
By Georgina Wilding

If love was the fluff between your toes
I'd leave it there.

Memories
By 'Aqilah Aziz

It came to my attention that if I write things down, my memories would flow from the tip of my pen and draw a picture on the canvas, turning it into a piece of fiction. I am in control of what I see, what I remember and what I feel.

I realized something had changed. I couldn't say it myself as I'd become impartial of it, but my writings had changed. Long gone were the gruesome effects of a knife killing pure souls with blood dripping from its edge. It had been replaced, smeared on the paper was not the sweet memories of happy collections, but the pain of the heart.

I wondered what happened between now and then, and all I could think of was your face. If, indeed, a writer's best weapon is his memory, then how long must this heartbroken warrior face the pain a soul has created? And a soul that doesn't even know it has inflicted this much rips in my heart nevertheless.

I had battled with my mind, refused to acknowledge the memories it flashed, refused to let my sword dance on the parchments as it would only singe the scars that still need healing. It had pained me that because of what I did, I lost my own war. The enemy hadn't even stepped a foot on the arena and I had blasted him. It was an unfair play committed by myself. I regretted everything.

I wished to believe I could change it, that I could recreate history and choose what could happen. But as an honest warrior, my pen refused to ink lies and dishonour my heart. And thus, even if this broken warrior had fallen, her stories would live.

And from the tip of my sword, I had become a different writer. I am in control of what I see, what I remember, but I have no control in what I feel.

Outskirts
By Andrew Henley

I turned the key in the ignition and drove off. The Kingdom of Blue Collar shrank in the rearview mirror as the beaks of the oil cranes pecked into the earth. The alkali flats were cracked like crème brûlée crust. My dance shoes vibrated on the backseat, steel heels clapping together. Applauding.

Light filled the car through the dusty windows. The shoes liked it. For so long they had been hidden in the back of the closet like a dirty magazine. It was not a town for dreamers. It was a town where men put food onto the table with their sweaty, callused palms and women cooked and cleaned. Nobody danced.

The Skyline
By Sanjana Parikh

Adventure, passion, speed and challenges. That's what I wanted from life. I never wanted to stop. I never wanted to turn and look back. I never wanted to have any regrets. I knew my life wouldn't stop at one place, one house or one country. I wanted change and I wanted fun.

When my Mom passed away, a part of me, which I knew would not be happy, wanted to stay home and take care of the house she had built. When I did talk to her about it, a few days before she left me, she said, "Oh, darling! I did not raise you to sit at home and '*take care of the house I built.'* It will always be there for you, Lisa, I will always be in that house when you miss me, and it's yours. But go, baby. Do what you want, do what makes you happy."

She made me promise to follow my heart, wherever it took me. She used to say, "The universe doesn't give you signs. Your heart does. The universe just helps you chase them." Before she died, she put something in my hand and asked me to keep it with me always.

"Ready, Lisa?" My instructor asked, and I switched back to the present.

I opened my palm and looked at the stone my Mom had given me. It was a small, pink coloured one. She called it her lucky stone. And I truly believed that it had kept me safe. I had survived difficult injuries when I had it with me. I was sure it had my Mother's soul in it. I put the stone in the pocket near my heart and got up.

"Yes, Sir, ready."

I went to the edge of the plane and closed my eyes as I murmured a small prayer. I opened my eyes, looked out into the infinity, and pushed myself off the plane. The wind gushed on my face as I floated in the sky. The land was 40,000 feet below me and my Mom was right in my heart.

London, Untouched
By Sara Assumani

I would say, mama, my love is like the ocean. Rise and fall, crash and roar, ebb and flow, mighty as it is – it'll seep through your fingers at the touch.

Perceptions of Feminism
By Kaya Gromocki

"I slept with a feminist the other night!" said this guy friend of mine. Apparently, the girl had wanted to be on top during their one night stand, an advocating symptom of her being a fully-fledged feminist. This ludicrous assumption got me thinking about the misconceptions surrounding feminism, as they exist in both the reality of university life and among my own generation. Wanting to explore the issue, I turned to a source that is as indisputable as the necessity of buying Tesco Value Everything during your short student life: a dictionary.

First, I looked up what light the Oxford Dictionary had to shed on this apparently sticky issue. In there, 'Feminism' reads as it follows: 'The advocacy of women's rights on the ground of the equality of the sexes'. Sounds simple enough. I decided to gather a few more descriptions before declaring the case closed. I turned to my own pocket-sized copy of the Collins English Dictionary. Once again, the definition is as simple as Paris Hilton's mind: 'The advocacy of equal rights for women'. Just to triple check it is really as straightforward as it seems, I browsed the Cambridge Dictionary Online too – and, would you believe it? Feminism is defined as 'the belief that women should be allowed the same rights, power, and opportunities as men and be treated in the same way'.

Because of these definitions, I can't help but feel that men and women alike who claim to not be feminists probably don't own a dictionary, or, if they do, they have never bothered to brush up on their vocabulary. Associating the word 'feminist' with the idea of a hairy, violent, bra-burning woman who wants to do away with the male population and feed their bodies to her herd of cats is just as flawed as calling someone who steals your bike from your front garden a 'cycles lover'. It is the equivalent of assuming your friend studying politics will end up lying and cheating and pretending to care about anything that is not their humongous monthly income as soon as they graduate.

Another common misconception is that feminists are just kicking up a fuss about nothing, because women like Emily Davison had already conquered equality in the 20s. Many people seem to believe that feminism is as much of use to society as their second cousins' daily Facebook updates. However, you only need to google 'I need feminism because' to see how current and relevant of an issue it is, in fervent need of a lot of work. If we don't need feminism, then why is it still an insult to refer to anyone as doing anything 'like a girl'? Or define anyone demonstrating cowardly behaviour as a 'pussy', while a brave individual would 'have balls'? Why is a man having frequent sex with different women still praised by his peers, and a woman behaving the same way is shamed and considered a slut? Why is the gender pay gap on an average of 15.7%? Why does it exist at all? In the Western world, these are some of the most basic and obvious questions highlighting the need for feminism. Sadly, these issues derive from beliefs and behaviours deeply ingrained in our society, our language and our values. There are lots of things to be done, but the first step you can take to make a difference is to not shake your head and laugh next time someone tells you they are a feminist. Instead, try saying 'me too', because believing your gender does not make you superior or inferior to anyone else is the starting point to turn it into a reality.

Enough

By Alexandra Adamson

Veins broken
from buried sins
and empty secrets.
Immune to the darkness
of lies,
a heart empty
of what gives it life.

Do You Mind
By Leigh Campbell

You see me shivering when it's cold outside
and open up the side of your coat;
an invitation for me
to sap you of your warmth
or bask in it.
I do not think you mind.

You drive the half-hour journey to my house
only to drive me away again.
despite the cost of petrol,
because you know what happens
when I'm left there too long.
I do not think you mind.

You stand up for me
while I lay on the ground.
I remain motionless
as you slay my demons.
I stand still, impassive,
as you wipe tears from my cheeks.
I do not think you mind.

You sit with me in the quiet,
my head resting on your shoulder
or chest
or knees.
Sometimes the silence seems to last forever.
I do not think you mind.

You hug me so tightly;
I hug back just as hard.
Sometimes I think that one day,
I will hold you so closely
you will cease to exist.
I do not think you would mind.

You pretend so well
that you are not angry,
or sad,
that you do not need help.
I hope you know that I can see right through you.
I hope you know that I do not mind.

Untitled (3)
By Uta Feinstein

The Mask In The Sky.
By Kwaku Asafu-Agyei.

The sunshine is his smile
to hide his sadness. The
stars are the sparks in his
eyes to let you know he still
possesses the key. The rain is
his tears to dilute the pain
and the moving cloud is his
tissue to soak up his tears.

Sunday Service
By Elizabeth Cooper

The train peels with blue patterned seats,
On the 10:46 Sunday service
From Brough to London Kings Cross.

A blonde haired man with a blood pocket eye
Is singing London's Burning
London's Burning
Fire, Fire
Fire, Fire

Grey glass sky. Rust red fox
Matted fur and bubble trail paw prints.
He pads along the cold train tracks
The sky leaks small droplets
That remain hanging in the air.

Coaches lean over an embankment
Circling neon, yellow workmen
With sewn on faces:
A lifeless engine.

London's Burning
London's Burning
Fire, Fire
Fire, Fire

No Visitors
By Andrew Henley

A tangled thorn bush of tubes consumes a hospital bed. Inside their plastic sarcophagus, at this stage as ornate as they are necessary, a man is trapped in medically induced purgatory.

The skin on his hands is thick like work gloves after a life of blue collar evolution. His old body retains the basic muscles of youth, now shrivelled and withering. A lifetime of sun and sweat has stained his complexion earthy maroon.

He has two children, no wife, and no visitors. His wife left him like a steamroller; it was slow, it was painful, it squeezed everything out of him and just left an imprint. The broken heart was a catalyst, the poison in his veins the puppet strings. The way he looked at his children. The way he pulled his arm back. The way he clenched his fist.

His daughter had her mother's smile.

His son had his mother's eyes.

He had two children and no visitors. Inside his nest of life-support, he flatlined.

R&B
By Uta Feinstein

Inspirations
By Charlotte Porter

Inspirations aren′t supposed to be summed up in words. Inspirations excel beyond mere fanciful idioms. They open a part of you that's usually cushioned by daily norms and the everyday hurdles that hinder us from seeing a brighter picture. Inspirations are what we make them to be. They can be anything; from a rhythmic drum beat accompanied by the strings of a ukulele, to the petty folds in the corner of a smile of that special someone. They free a dynamic vehemence, invoking a passion we never knew we had. They drive an explosion of motivation; words bursting onto a blank piece of paper, colours surging onto a stretch of white wall, or music flowing melodiously from parted lips.

I was ten when I first went to Nusa Lembongan. Arriving in Bali, first time or not, it's obvious to see the way things work. Even now, you're absorbed into this stereotypical mannerism. There's an unspoken yet mandatory uniform of flip flops and a comfy pair of freelance shorts, complimented with the Bali-branded Bintang shirt. I know I've fallen under the spell, thinking that adopting the appearance is the customary prototype whilst ignoring the underlying feeling that it's all a pretence. It's almost as if Bali has been swallowed by a pseudo culture of foreigners in flimsy furnish under the impression they're living in a paradise, and that it's their paradise. The throngs of crowds that flock into the airport never cease, no matter what time of year. The air is thick with the smell of sunscreen: a pollution that erodes the Balinese culture as it crumbles into nothing.

Cynical judgments aside, getting on the boat to the remote island of Nusa Lembongan is different. It's a platitude, but as you watch the mainland fade into mere pencil shades of grey, you leave behind the vexatious stereotypes. As the bow of the speedboat bounces ferociously over the sea, cutting into the pulsing waves rolling past, you know you're approaching a different side to Bali. Getting off the boat, you can almost sense the difference in atmosphere. On an island less laden with tourists, you're outnumbered by the locals. As it should be; this is their home, you are their guest. I've heard the tales of Bali in its glory, during the days when Seminyak's Jalan 66 was merely a road to the beach where some chose to sell souvenirs for the few that visited. Now it's a famed shopping strip, renowned for beer shirts and the tie-dye beach dresses craved by most Westerners. I may be a bit of a sceptical scrooge but I'm at the point where I'm almost embarrassed by my own culture, convinced that there is an underlying hostility behind the Balinese charm that smiles and thanks you for paying a price that suited *you* on *your* terms; for replacing their culture with fast food restaurants and shopping malls; for transforming peaceful postcard beaches into a maze of parasols and beds and red lobster-like legions.

Not to say that Nusa Lembongan doesn't have its share of tourism. The beachfront has developed a strip of wooden villas with straw roofs and personalized swimming pools. Day-trips from the mainland are especially popular; one of which, definitely being my favourite, attracts those who simply can't decide whether it's worth it to remove their makeup if they want to swim with the fish. So instead, they've combined the two by inventing an underwater space suit, equipped with a glass dome head that prevents your mascara from smudging whilst you plod along the sandy bottom. That aside, the culture in Lembongan is still preserved, and hopefully permanent. Past the tourist façade, you're able to see into the soul of Lembongan. Bumping over the decaying roads on a battered motorbike, you can drive for hours through serene jungle roads and dirt tracks along the coast, exploring the labyrinth of roads that entice you into the island's heart. I've read novels and listened to songs that speak about the feeling of being alive, but only after I experienced the exhilarating rush of racing under a kaleidoscope of shadows formed by a tunnel of trees did I really understand what they meant.

I could pretend that I'm one of those people who will voluntarily hike up a mountain just for a breathing taking view, but I'm not. Yet putting my suitcase down by the foot of the bed and standing by the window, breathing in a fresh, salty sea breeze, I could be. My bedroom window looks like a painted picture frame: Mount Agun erects on the mainland in the distance, glazed by a thin layer of cloud and haze. The ocean is sandwiched by a layer of lush jungle and a tranquil blue sky. I hold my breath, waiting for the familiar Vietnamese soundtrack of distant car horns and raspy motorbike exhausts, or perhaps the feedback of some karaoke machine, or the neighbour's dog that never seem to stop barking. Instead I hear the low rumble of waves, accompanied by a choir of chirps or an orchestra of crickets. I hear the sounds of leaves passing secrets and the wooden frames of my window sighing. It's – what's the word we don't often use when we live in the heart of Hanoi – peaceful.

Nusa Lembongan is notorious for diving. Brought up in a family of keen divers, we're always game for the opportunity, even if it means battling with a resisting wetsuit. My favourite place to dive is Manta Point on the other side of Nusa Penida. The boat turns into an opening in the cliff-face, into a small chasm filled with clear, crystal-like water. Subsequently, we all proceed to throw ourselves overboard and sink like water logged feathers. The swell caused from the waves crashing into the rock face on the surface creates an underwater dance floor: we all sway side to side in a subaquatic waltz, our tubes and regulators hanging like tassels to our waterproof ball gowns. You swim to a point where the sandbank drops away and forms a kind of bowl. Coral towers like skyscrapers, the tips reaching out like fingers trying to touch the surface. Shoals of silvery fish glint in the sun's rays. Larger fish chase each other, dodging and swerving around the coral, the water sliding gracefully over their long, slippery, sleek bodies. Pink, orange and rose-coloured sea anemones sway in a peaceful current. Several lion fish drift steadily by. A massive turtle rests in the shelter of a cave. Its shell is cracked and grooved with a lifetime of adventures and experiences. All of a sudden you'll fall into a shadow, eclipsed by a winged cloak as it flies overhead – so close that you can almost count the scars and unique markings on its smooth white belly. They soar; they glide; they spiral: the manta rays have arrived to feed.

Growing up overseas, I don't have a place to call home. Whilst my passport declares my British nationality and I've memorized the first two lines to *God Save the Queen*, I know that I'm as much of an outsider as a tourist on holiday. So when I'm welcomed by the waiter who works at the café with the kittens who play in the bathroom at the back because he remembers that I like plain pancakes with lemon and sugar, or the dive master remembers how I used to look when I first came to Nusa Lembongan when I was ten, it does make it feel like home. When I'm waiting for the ten 'o' clock boat on the mainland and I'm sitting with perhaps a French couple or an Australian family, I can't supress the feeling of superiority that I probably know the island better than them. It's not a crime to pretend that it's my island, because I discovered it in my own way and I turned it into my inspiration.

Brother

By Sean Keenan

My brother won't stop screaming and shouting in the middle of the night, it's keeping me up, making me agitated and short with people. I visited his grave and asked him to stop, but he won't listen.

Split Ends
By Eleanor Hemsley

Hello,

We've been together for a while now,
I feel like you're suddenly breaking away.
I used to be quite attached to you,
But now

I'm not so sure.

I think we need to break up,
Leave each other.
I need to cut myself
Off
From you.
I need a fresh start.

I'm sorry,
You need to go.
Tomorrow morning
At half past nine.

But for now,
Let's just enjoy our
Last night together.

Lots of love,
Layla.

Warmth. Haemorrhage. Connection. Death.
By Andrew Henley

Gerald and Lucinda were seaweed, anchored to a nasty little town called New Prysville. They were born there, they would die there. Small town mentality. It was the only home they'd ever known. New Prysville was a seaweed shark, playful and harmless to most things, but it tore Gerald and Lucinda apart.

Gerald and Lucinda worked at the mortuary. The people of New Prysville were suspicious of them, a married couple like that, working so close to death. What must they get up to? Every visit to the store warranted strange looks. Suspicious looks. Everybody wished funerals would just... happen. Without Gerald and Lucinda needing to do it. People *really* started talking three years ago, when 12 year old little Anna-Marie Johnson was murdered in New Prysville. They caught the guy that did it, Jim Manners, who voluntarily confessed. He had no connection to Gerald or Lucinda.

Anna-Marie's death was the biggest thing that ever happened to New Prysville. Second biggest was when a former resident came fourth in a national hot dog eating contest. Anne-Marie was pretty and young and female. Her murder was national news. International even, with her funeral broadcast live over the internet. Anna-Marie's mother, Charlaine Johnson, wore a red dress and a cubic zirconium necklace to the funeral. She told Gerald and Lucinda that she wanted her daughter's hair to look 'big and gorgeous, like that pop singer Lady Gigi'.

Anna-Marie was a pageant regular. Charlaine created Anna-Marie, and not just in the mother-daughter way. Everything thing about Anna-Marie was engineered to win every beauty pageant she entered. She was starved on a strict diet to give her a teenage figure. Baton-twirling was to be practised every day. Her mother painted her face, but Anna-Marie was less a canvas and more a palette. Just make up in its raw form.

Long, fake eyelashes, glitter on her cheeks, hair sprayed up like blonde whipped cream.

Gerald and Lucinda inevitably got Anna-Marie's hair wrong. She looked beautiful, in a peaceful sort of way. Her browning blonde locks were full and straight. They rested with dignity on her petite shoulders. But Charlaine kicked up a stink. And when Charlaine Johnson kicked up a stink, you could smell it three towns over and the clouds were toxic. She started shouting that Gerald and Lucinda were perverts, that they had desecrated her daughter (how Charlaine Johnson knew a word like 'desecrated' was anyone's guess), and even that they were in cahoots with Jim Manners. No truth and no proof. But shit sticks in a town like New Prysville.

For a couple of months after the funeral, Charlaine Johnson personally boycotted Gerald and Lucinda's funeral home. She didn't have any more dead daughters to aid her cause, so she just stood outside the door shouting at people that the place was run by sickos, and that God fearing regular folk should not give them time of day. Business did fall, but that was more because people were scared of Charlaine rather than Gerald and Lucinda.

After those couple of months, the people of New Prysville's shock over Anna-Marie Johnson wore off. There was no more publicity, so Charlaine stopped her campaign. And without Charlaine shrieking in their ears, it was quiet enough for people to think. Gerald and Lucinda *were* always a bit strange, weren't they? And only strange people spent that much time with dead bodies. Gerald and Lucinda had chosen a profession that meant they had unlimited access to dead bodies. Strange people. Dead bodies. And Anna-Marie *was* a very nice looking young girl. Pretty little girls with long hair and makeup, who would never fight it nor talk back. It didn't take much of a leap. Charlaine Johnson liked the sound of her own voice, that was for sure. Maybe she did talk sense though. That girl Rebecca Harrison who died in that car crash, she looked different at the funeral, didn't she? Had they done something to her? And maybe it wasn't just young girls. People gave Gerald and Lucinda a wide berth after that. They still got some business, but people never looked them in the eye.

Unlike Anna-Marie, Lucinda did not have hair that was blonde and full and straight. Her hair was black and wiry and knotted, with the texture of a retired drummer's beard. She envied the people whose hair she cut, and not just for their hair. Lucinda's skin was white, more corpse than china. She sometimes compared herself to the bodies the way friends do after a sunny holiday, and did not always come off favourably. Her mother once told her she looked like and English rose, but she had no cheekbones, and as far as she knew, no English blood. Those who were kind to Lucinda would say she had light blue eyes, but the people of New Prysville called them as grey. Gerald thought they were blue.

Gerald's hair was not wiry, but aside from that it was hard to tell what it was. It was black and constantly slicked back, and gave him a not un-snake-like appearance. His skin was light and fair, though not as much as Lucinda's. In fact, Gerald's skin tone would have looked quite pretty on Lucinda, but it did not suit a man. Lucinda called his eyes green, New Prysville called them yellow. The truth was somewhere in between.

Gerald and Lucinda drove their Camaro slowly up to the top of the hill on the South side of town. From there they could look out not only over New Prysville, but the neighbouring towns too. The ones still trying to wash Charlaine Johnson's stink off their clothes. Johnny Cash crackled on the radio as they came to a stop. They climbed into the backseat and began to undress. They were newly naked, not yet touching, as Johnny Cash metamorphosed into Lady Gaga. The radio told them to Just Dance though bouts of static and Lucinda sobbed against Gerald's bare chest as he stroked her hair. The thin sprouts of his chest hair became entangled in her long locks. Outside, a thunder clap and a lightning fork. They happened close together, almost on top of one another. Lucinda dragged Gerald out of the car.

They were naked, they were hairy and they were a little bit cold, but they didn't care. It was fall, so the huge looming tree that watched over New Prysville was down to its branches. The tree had borne witness to everything that had ever happened in New Prysville. The tree knew the truth.

Underneath the tree, they kissed. Gerald's hands held the milky pearls of Lucinda's breasts. Lucinda ran her fingers down the bumps of his spine.

"I want to be a part of you, but I don't want to be a part of this town."

Lightning stuck them. Warmth. Haemorrhage. Connection. Death. Their bodies merged. They were fused at the hips, the skin bare and flat like Barbie and Ken. A real glamour couple. The surge of electricity had engulfed the two of them into one entity. Their faces had been kissing, and their mouths and noses disappeared as the bolt of lightning melted them together. Their eyelids were soldered shut. Their skin was bubbled and looked as though it were welded along a pink seam. It was impossible to tell which of them was Lucinda and which was Gerald. They would be a part of each other forever. They were free.

Breaking the Mould
By Sean Keenan

The most powerful and difficult thing a writer does is to project their mind onto a page and let others judge it.

Strong Stomach
By Kimberly Jamison

She expertly breaks the ribcage,
Cracking as she goes.
She uses a chainsaw
To carve a smile into the bones.

She's more restrained than last time,
And doesn't finger the aorta
But continues with the job.
Take a right, avoid the liver.

The lungs are still attached
So the scalpel is the tool.
Incision next to the sternum,
Lift the organs out,
Slipping her hands in like a hug
It makes a '*shhhliickkk*' sound.

This time she doesn't pass out and
Her vision stays clear
Despite the sweltering room.
Odd, because there are corpses in here.

She cleans up and scrubs down
In a mist of preservative
Then heads straight out to lunch.
Quick as you like
To be first in line
Because today is Spaghetti Bolognaise.

Silent Witness
By Helen Raven

Lou couldn't reach. She gritted her teeth and strained her arm, standing on her tip toes. Feeling the chair beneath her wobble, she struggled to keep her balance. She only wanted the tin of biscuits. Bella had told her this morning that if she behaved herself while she popped out to meet a friend she could have her special chocolate cookie cream biscuits. Bella had always kept her promises. Though this time she had forgotten to get the biscuit tin down, which meant she had to get them herself and she was adamant to get them, Lou had earned those biscuits.

She could see the pink and red spotty tin. She could almost touch it with her fingertips but every time she did so, it seemed to push further away from her. She could always wait until Bella got back but she didn't know how long Bella would be and her mother was at work. She wasn't due back until eight. Lou couldn't wait that long. She was hungry.

A sudden idea hit her. She stepped up onto the marble surface, stood up straight and reached up to the top shelf of the cupboard. Why Bella had to keep her biscuit tin up on the top shelf, she'd never know. What was the point? Bella herself couldn't even reach it without standing on a chair or getting mum to reach it for her. Lou pulled a face, her tongue stuck out between her teeth in concentration and stretched up even harder, but she still couldn't reach the tin.

She heard the front door open and breathed a sigh of relief. Bella was home. She could get them down for her. Lou didn't want her to know that she'd been trying to get them though, so quickly she closed the cupboard door. Then she heard voices. She froze. That wasn't Bella. She listened hard, heart thumping against her ribcage faster and faster. It was her mother, but she couldn't place the other voice. It was a male's voice that didn't sound like daddy. Being careful not to make any noise, Lou stepped back down on the chair and safely onto the floor. She managed to pick the chair up and put it back at the table where she'd got it from. She stood in the middle of the kitchen and listened to the voices in the hall way.

"We've had this argument too many times," came her mother's voice.

"I know, but you never give me an answer."

"That's because it's difficult, Adam, I have two kids, a husband..."

"Hang on, are you sure it's safe to be here?" asked the unknown male's voice.

"Rob's not back from work until six, and Isabelle said she was taking Louanna to the park today, so the house is empty," replied her mother.

Lou's eyes widened. Why would Bella lie about that? And what was her mother doing back from work with another man that wasn't her father?

"I just want to know where I stand with you, Jennifer." The man's voice sounded edgy. The voices were getting closer and they were heading towards the kitchen.

Lou glanced around the kitchen in a panic. She had to find somewhere to hide. She saw the bottom cupboard, next to the one under the sink. It was always kept empty, and she was small enough to hide in it. She'd done it before. It was the hiding place she always chose when playing hide and seek. She dashed for the cupboard, climbed inside and closed the door but not all the way; she left a slither of light so she could see.

Just as she climbed inside, the kitchen door opened and from her hiding place, Lou saw her mother walk in, dressed in her smart, navy suit which she had left the house in this morning. She was talking.

"Look, it's not that I don't enjoy spending time with you, I do. We have fun, don't we? We enjoy each other's company, so why do you have to spoil it by bringing my bloody husband in to the equation?" She sat down at the table. The man walked towards the cupboard in which she was hiding. Lou shrank back in fear of being found out. Who was this man in her house?

"I need a drink."

"There's some cider in the fridge." He headed towards the fridge and opened it, taking out one of daddy's bottles of beer instead. No one was allowed to drink them but daddy. Lou watched in complete awe as the man paced up and down the kitchen floor in front of her, opening and closing drawers looking for something. She couldn't see his face, but he didn't seem to be dressed in a suit. He was wearing jeans that were frayed and dirty at the bottom.

"Where's the bottle opener?" he asked finally. He was standing right in front of her. She held her breath, scared that he would hear her.

"In the drawer below the cupboard over there."

The man moved from in front of her, and Lou was able to see her mother again, still sitting at the table, her legs crossed elegantly – red painted nails tapping gently against the wood.

"Adam, why are you getting so worked up about this? It hasn't bothered you before. You knew what you were getting yourself into when we first started."

"I knew you were married, I knew you had two children, but you told me your marriage was dead."

"Yeah, what's your point?"

"I saw you together. You looked happy with one another, you know, like there was no one else in the world but you two."

"It's all an act, Adam," replied her mother. "We're still together because of *our* children," she said, putting emphasis on the word 'our'.

The man scoffed. "Oh please, when was the last time you spent any time with your children?"

There was a sudden change of atmosphere and a long silence. Lou shrank back into the cupboard further, terrified that maybe they'd realized she was listening in.

"What's that supposed to mean?"

"You know exactly what that's supposed to mean. If you're not with me, then you're at work and if you're not there, you're out socialising with your so-called friends attending cocktail parties with your husband." The man's voice grew louder as he got angrier. "Face it, Jennifer; you don't spend any time with your children at all."

"How dare you?" Her mother stood up from the table, her eyes were narrowed and her red lips had disappeared into a straight line; just like they did every time she was in danger of losing her temper.

"What? It's the truth. You know full well you hardly ever see them. When was the last time you spent the day with your two girls?"

Silence.

"My eldest is fifteen; she doesn't want to be seen spending the day with her mother at her age. She likes to do her own thing." Her mum spoke quietly as if trying to reassure herself as well as the man.

But the man just laughed, yet there was no humour behind it. It was dry, tasteless and sent chills down Lou's spine. She shivered, letting a small noise escape from her lips. She clamped a hand across her mouth in case she'd been heard.

"Yes, but your youngest is seven, am I correct? She wants nothing more than to spend time with her mother."

"And how do you know what my daughter wants?" demanded her mum. "Louanna doesn't know what she wants. If she wanted to see me she'd talk, she'd tell me that herself, but she doesn't, she doesn't speak to anyone. Not even me. Do you know how that makes me feel? I have a daughter who suffers from selective mutism. She doesn't tell me how much she loves me, she doesn't tell me that she wants to see me, or spend time with me. So don't you dare stand there and lecture me on spending time with my children when you don't know the first thing about my family."

Lou sat watching in her hiding place in complete awe, she never knew her mum felt like that about her. She loved her mum. Of course she did. She adored her mother, and wouldn't want her to be upset.

"Is that why you don't spend time with them?"

"I want you to leave now."

"I don't understand you, Jennifer," said the man, his voice softening slightly. "If you're not happy, then just leave."

"I can't just leave."

"Why not? Let's run away together, just the two of us. We'd be happy together."

Lou's eyes opened wide, as she took in what was being said. She wanted run out from her hiding place, cling on to her mother, shouting no, she didn't want her to leave. She wanted to tell her that she did love her. She drew a picture of them together just the other day, with the words 'I love you, mummy' written in red crayon. She had got Bella to stick it up on the fridge so her mother would see it.

"I'm not leaving."

"Jen..."

"I'd like you to leave now." She cleared her throat. "And I don't think we should see each other again."

"Are you ending it?"

Her mother said nothing. Even Lou knew that that was a no. Mummy always said nothing when she meant no.

"Oh no, no, no, no, you can't finish it with me," the man's voice was beginning to get louder again. "We're happy together; you know that, you can't just throw away what we have just because you're too scared to leave your husband."

"Throw away what we have?" her mother repeated. "What are you talking about, Adam? *We*," Lou watched as her mother walked up to the man, shaking her finger between the two of them, "don't have anything. We never have. It was just sex, Adam. I like to live dangerously. I like a challenge. I was never going to leave my husband for you, I thought you knew that."

“You really are a cold hearted bitch, aren’t you?”

“Well, how was I to know that you were going to go all puppy-eyed and desperate on me.” She turned her back on him. “Now, please leave. I don’t want to see you again.”

The silence that followed was deafening. Lou peered through the crack in the cupboard door, just wishing that someone would speak or leave. Yes, she wanted the man to leave.

Out of nowhere, the man raised his arm above his head, Lou caught sight of the beer bottle still in his hand. Before Lou could work out what was happening, the bottle smashed against her mother’s temple, penetrating it with pieces of glass. Lou put a hand to her mouth to stifle her own gasp, moving forward in the cupboard. As if in slow motion, her mum’s back stiffened, and then subsided to the floor; knocking her head against the table as she went down. Lou stared in horror as her mum lay on the floor. She shrank even further back into the cupboard. She could still see what was going on. She could see the man’s legs. She watched as he crouched down beside her mum.

“Jen...” His voice was quiet. “Jen, come on, don’t die on me.”

“Mum?” Bella’s voice drifted through the kitchen. Lou couldn’t see her. She wanted to scream out. She wanted to yell out, kick her legs to make any sort of sound that would warn Bella that she was here, but she was too afraid. “Oh my... who the hell are you?”

“Stay where you are,” barked the man, getting to his feet. *Run, Bella, run away before he gets you too* screamed the voice inside Lou’s head. *RUN.* “Hey, I said stay where you are!”

Lou watched as the man left the kitchen. She heard the front door bang against the wall and then silence. Her heart was pounding against her chest. What had she just witnessed? She wanted to scream. She wanted to yell. Let people know what she had just seen. She tried, but no words came out.

Duties Call
By T.R.J. Shelley

Bullets fly

Twisted and callous
They pierce the sky

Fast forward into the night
Lighting up a torrid sight

A city formerly filled with hopes and dreams
Torn asunder by the fall of once steady beams

As bombs explode and shrapnel glides
Slicing straight through metal street signs

BANG BANG
More bullets fly
They whiz and crack as soldiers die

Cowards run
And heroes fall
Consigned to the merciless fate
Of duties call

Descending Snowfall
By Kaya Gromocki

Taken in Alderly Edge, Cheshire

Where or What is Strength.
By Kwaku Asafu-Agyei

Is strength in the fists of a boxer?
Or in the legs of an athlete?

Is strength seen in a tree with bark?
Or in water that propels an ocean?

Is it something found
In a rock built on solid grounds?
Or in an educational institution; with principle?

Is strength found in the mind?
Or beneath the ground that I walk upon?

Is it assembled in an electric cable?
Or in an engine that energizes a vehicle?

Is it knowledge?
Is it beauty?
Is it just a word?

To me;
True strength
Is found
Within.

Rainy Day
By Eliza Gradwohl

Skies cry
Clouds dance by
Puddles form on the street
Rivers travel on concrete
I stand outside
My arms held high
Rejoicing.

Skies cry
I sigh
Happy and sad at one time
Cleansed of all my grime
My mind clean as a slate
As I just sit and wait
Relaxing.

Skies cry
I say goodbye
My feet are stomping and sloshing
Covered by my galoshes
I am wet, no soaked
Still I have provoked
Imagination.

Skies cry
As do my eyes
As the pen hits the page
I'm released from my cage
Free.

Blossom
By Kimberly Jamison

She is the type of beauty
that you'd see in blossom petals
stuck to the road
after it's rained.
The crushed pink litter, no longer
perfect but still delicate and pretty.
In the back of your mind
as you walk over this fragile
blushing carpet,
you know it will only remain this way
for a finite time.

Because now she's wearing short skirts
drinking Jack from the bottle
trying to shed her
public school wings.
She wants to be badder than the best
so takes another swig
downing her etiquette
sitting in the way
her teachers told her in no circumstance a lady
should sit.
The air is thick with ash and sweat,
she rejects her background with
a long drag
from a short fag
blunt, brittle, varnish chipped.
She'll seek solace in a man who's not to be trusted
a year ago
she'd have been disgusted.
But right now this night will either end
with a strong black Nescafé
or plan B
from a judgemental pharmacy.

The girl she was
is so different
from the girl she is
but only the strongest will tell her this.
On one long night
when they've all had enough
they'll sit under those cherry trees
she'll tell them the story of how her heart broke,
the secret she keeps so far inside
she now needs help to reach it.
They'll know why she felt the need to change
into this grotesque caricature
this ugly shell she calls home.

She'll hear those words she's been looking for
forgiveness will chase the cold from her bones.
They'll go inside when it starts to rain
nothing miraculous will happen,
the world will not be changed.
But the course of a life will be altered in such a way
that its importance will reverberate
in family tales
the memories will always bring a smile
to an old woman's face
the delicate wrinkles outlining the years she spent laughing.
She'll die knowing that she was worth the time
because even as it rains
the droplets of water
that now land on the tree
make the soft petals so heavy
that they can't take the weight of the rain.
So they are dragged down to the pavement.
They become bent, broken.

But nonetheless, they remain
Beautiful.

Hare Series 3 – Untitled #1
By Lydia Crump

An Open Wound Closed the Door
By Georgina Wilding

An open wound closed the door
I never got to find out if that plate scarred.

Meant To Be
By Natasha Keates

The sharp scent of the numb autumn wind.
Golden leaves swirled through the breeze,

And we sat together.

A lavender haze graced the sky.
The ripples on the water had faded,
and now we could breathe clear.

My head rested on your shoulder
whilst we watched the world turn.

The ice metal bar in the curve of my back.
The comfiest I'd ever been.

Your chest rose and fell
and we listened to the trickle of the fountain.

I looked up at your smiling face
as my fake cheeks ached.

A beam of light lit the tips of the clouds,
shining through the gaps like yellow fog.

For a moment we focussed on the beauty together,
But I knew your thoughts had changed.

Even though you're here with me,
I know you're somewhere else.

You're sitting by the beach with her,
Drawing shapes in the sand.

Tracing her frosty snow white skin,
Tucking a strand of chestnut hair safely behind her ear.

Admiring each other,
Instead of gazing at the world.

For your sky will be cloudless, the purest of blue,
as you sit with her, and I sit with you.

Shrinking World, Expanding Lungs
By Andrew Henley

Hammering hands, red raw fists
knock on a
tightly
closed door. No answer yet
from dirt and death.

Splinters dig into soft
untouched flesh under fingernails; bite
like a broken key's
teeth in a pre-emptive
coffin.

Twine bracelets,
clothes honey yellow
with sweat. Blood jewellery,
ruby earrings. Choked
by a fictional necklace,

air stuck
in the throat like vomit. Inhaling
darkness and dirt.
Shrinking world,
expanding lungs.

Mini avalanche
of dust, black
sky slowly
falling.
Fallen.

Last words,
last breath.
"Sorry,"
as it always should
be.

Untitled (5)
By Uta Feinstein

Drunk

By Sean Keenan

I've just gotten back from the night,
Feelings are dashing, feels so right
I reach for the door
It slips

I walk through the darkness of the house I'm in,
Stumbling, reaching, my head's in a spin
I sit in the sofa
It slips

I talk to myself as I climb to my feet
Begin to feel woozy fall back on the seat
I get up once more
And head for the door
It slips

At the kitchen sink, drinking water's my goal
It's a fair price to pay for poisoning my soul
I lean over and see
The drink I had earlier
It slips

It's a hint I think for me to find
To stop the intoxicating of my mind
But I can't help it I just want some more
I'm getting pretty friendly with the kitchen floor
It slips

It's late or is it early yet?
The drink will help me to forget
The memories of my past

And finally be at peace with myself, at last
I slip

Risk Taking
By Liam Powell

Here we were again, sucking us in once more, like a Dyson on full blast. When was the last time I managed to just walk past a Casino? God knows, I don't. It's been a while, I know that much. This place has the potential to make your week – it also has the potential to break it. That was a more likely scenario.

Me and Dennis must have 'Mugs' written on our foreheads. Back again for the fourth time in as many days, when was the last time we won? That's right, we haven't. They say gambling's a mug's game. It's worse than that. Get too drawn in and it can ruin your life, and it doesn't take long either.

I've seen broken men walk out of those doors. Men who've lost everything they had, all because they'd been thick enough to try and double it. I walk out when I'm ahead, the only trouble being that it doesn't happen often. Last week I won a hundred, the next day I lost two hundred. That's how this game goes: sooner or later, the Casino always wins.

The place itself is plain. A few tables of Roulette, one or two for cards, which me and Dennis can't play for our lives, and a bar at the end. That's another rip-off. Four quid for a bottle of beer – I was stunned when the girl first told me – but who the hell am I to say no? You need the beer to keep yourself in this place, otherwise you'd sober up and realize you're a dumbass for being here. And of course I couldn't be having that. Sense is one thing every gambler has in common – none of it that is. Every time you see another tenner disappear, normal people would say enough is enough. Gamblers don't. Out comes a twenty, and let's win it all back. Smart idea.

"A quick bet?" asked Dennis, as we tried to just stroll past the place.

“Why not?” I could think of a hundred answers to my own question, yet none of them could make me see sense. That was something that losing £100 could do so much more effectively.

“Roulette?” As if we were going to do anything different.

Me and Dennis flash our membership cards to the girl at the desk, and proceed to almost certainly lose our money. The waitresses give us a nod as we walk in. We know them all. That’s a depressing thought, being in this place so often that not a single member of staff is unfamiliar.

We get to the table and put down our coats. Change the cash into chips, and let’s go. This time will be different, can’t lose every time. Lost fifty last night, that’s history. Win it back tonight, and then something extra for luck.

“Place your bets.” This bloke must love working here. Seeing hundreds of men, and a fair few women, chuck their hard earned money away – many of them repeatedly, like myself and Dennis – and just watching their faces fall. Of course you get winners, but they’re outnumbered. Every time.

“What you thinking?” I asked Dennis.

“Black,” I copied his move, and watched as the ball inevitably landed on red.

“Black again.”

Seven red didn’t look black to me. Time to try a different tact. Let’s go for the odds-evens now. Better luck there, must be. Not sure why, the chances are exactly the same.

“Evens.” Of course it was odds.

“Odds.”

This time we were confident. The ball didn't care that we were, plonking itself onto an even. Twenty lost in five minutes. How many times have I thought that this week?

"Let's win it back!" Great idea, Dennis. We put another twenty on the table, double or nothing. This can only end well. We put the lot on black. Watching that ball spin is agonising, pleading that it goes your way. Come on, black!

Red.

"Fuck this, let's go." That's the best idea we've had since we got here. Coats in our hands, heads slightly bowed, we walk silently to the exit. Some call the morning-after a one-night stand the walk of shame. That's nothing compared to this. Leave a girl's house the morning after and leave a Casino when you've lost big and tell me which feels worse.

"Let's leave the Casino's alone, now."

Fat chance.

Servant.
By Keira Andrews

The sapphire cape cascaded behind the young woman as her heeled shoes clattered against the stone floor. Throughout the corridor, wooden doors slammed against their feeble frames, whilst trapped air whistled through the thin gaps within the wall. The lady spared a moment's glance over her shoulder, before diving towards a large door to her left. The wind howled at an increased pace, and the woman grabbed the raised railings of the wooden bridge to remain standing. The courtyard had never seemed so far below.

The cape twisted around the woman's legs; slicing against her sides and encouraging her stray hairs to knot themselves in the wind's dance. Yet the woman didn't seem to notice. She didn't pause to look at the drop, or to look back over her shoulder at the following guards. The woman just stood there. Her gaze trapped on the narrow indent in the bridge's centre.

Small enough to not be given a second thought.

Large enough for a young child to hide from their daily chores.

It was the place where they had first met as children. The place they had spoken to each other in a manner unbefitting their social station. The place they thought it was impossible to be overheard. The place that, all these years later, they were taken from. The woman was never given the chance to say goodbye.

The wind roared at the woman's indifference, and tore strands of hair from her neat, plaited hold in its anguish. Locks of hair tumbled over her shoulders and flew about her face; each strand slapping against her skin like the edge of a whip, tearing away from her scalp with sharp, shooting pains. The air's moans drowned her ears in misery, like the sound of a mother wailing for her lost child.

The woman idly wondered, as she looked how far the stone courtyard was below, if Leon's mother had cried with as much pain as Nature's breath did now. Mother Nature, herself, crying out at the injustice of the deed.

The young woman couldn't recall allowing her voice to howl alongside the wind, but now the noise ripped from her throat like a starved beggar hunting for food.

The darkness of the starless night pressed against the woman's lids, like a blanket of smothering isolation. Yet, instead, the lady could only see the cropped red strands of hair under the summer's glare.

She could hear the squeak of muddy boots against the polished floor.

She could feel the rough hands as they secretly held hers.

She could picture the dimples in each cheek as a wide grin stretched across the face that she loved.

She could see the mischievous glint hidden behind large blue eyes.

She could see Leon.

And it hurt.

Her hands were pale under the moon's light. It was a full moon. It was their moon. When the rest of the castle hid away as they teased one another with folktales of werewolves and spirits of the night – yet made sure their doors were bolted closed. It was when they thought they could never be seen. It was when they thought they had been safe.

A large pair of hands appeared from behind her; the following guards having finally pushed open the correct door. The woman had no more screams left to give, and allowed her body to be wrestled from the side of the bridge.

It was with a detached thought that she noted how she had climbed onto the railing, and that the wind had been giving her the gentle push. A push that meant falling. A push that meant death. A push that meant Leon.

And suddenly she was fighting. She was fighting to jump.

"She's mad!" yelled a stranger's voice in her ear. Another pair of hands appeared at her feet, each one grasping an ankle with a firm, unwavering grip. The lady was carried back into the corridor of slamming frames and whistles of the storm outside. She was thrown unceremoniously onto the floor.

Her sobs sent shudders through each limb, and her breath rattled her bones as if accompanying an orchestra of sound in the night. She wanted to curl into a ball. She wanted to throw herself off the bridge. She wanted her Leon. Yet most of all, she wanted to forget – just for a moment – to know what it was like to love… so that she never need know what it is to have lost.

"Lady Ariana." A set of knees appeared by her body. "Lady Ariana." The woman made no response; she let her tears be her words and her breath be her voice. "Go get the Physician, and you, inform Lord George."

Two sets of footsteps sped away. Lady Ariana became aware of a heavy hand on her shoulder. Comforting her. Containing her. "What's wrong with the lady, d'ya reckon?" A young man, who Ariana recognized to be a guard, sniffed.

There was a pause. "It must be that servant." The two men talked as if Ariana wasn't present.

"Servant?" The younger man paused. "Which servant?"

"You know," the older man sighed, "the one that got whipped and quartered."

"But why would *she* be upset?" The guard replied. "That servant was always odd. Never thought they'd of tried to kiss the little lady though. Deserved it, righ'?"

"Yes." Came the sharp reply. "Unnatural, disgusting act. We can only hope the devil didn't fly from the servant and into our lady."

"Ya re'kon that's what it is, then?" Ariana heard the scuffle of a pair of boots stepping away.

"That's for the Court Physician to decide." The kneeling man stood up. "Let's hope the devil was chased away by the whipping. I heard it took hours for the servant to die."

The woman tensed – her teeth grating together and her fists so tight that her nails split the skin. It was the way they talked about *the servant* that angered her most.

Ariana could picture Leon being dragged to the whipping post. Her father had insisted that she watch every stroke. Leon's apron soaked some of the blood from the floor – the ties hanging lose over Leon's hips.

It was the only time Ariana had seen Leon in a dress.

They had been caught.

A royal and a peasant.

A lady and a servant girl.

Leona to all.

Leon to her.

Unnatural, the guard had said.

Devil's work, her father had spat.

Love, she had whispered as each lash beat against the servant girl's back.

Most Colours
By Uta Feinstein

Frozen
By Elisa Gradwohl

I froze
Yet time moved on.
People changed: grew and died,
Yet I remained.

My arms suspended
Forever lying to the world.
How sad can life be
When one's purpose is taken away?

People change,
Yet I remain the same.
The scenery, the environment,
It all adapts.

But I am left as me.
Frozen, forever, in the universe.
Alone, forgotten, unnoticed.
To watch forever
And never reawaken.

Entrapment
By Sean Keenan

I'm asking you, please don't resent me
It's not my fault you're empty.
But I know I'm loved enough for two
Even if that doesn't include you.

I have this tattoo in pink and blue
It's almost like the one on you,
My eyes in here are half focussed
And yet I see more than you do.

They put me here against my will
Surrounded by walls of loneliness.
I know you care, but He doesn't
For reasons of his own selfishness.

You touch me so tender with a smile
And whisper how you love me so.
He's not coming to see me, I sigh
But in features I can't let him go.

Mother, you were driven to the cliff;
You stared outwards and into the abyss.
I wish I could speak, oh the things I would say

Please don't let it end this way.

You went to the edge and induced me out;
I was screaming you've done the wrong thing.
You said you loved me, but you're such a liar
As my first and last breath is engulfed in the fire.

Stuck
By Kimberly Jamison

Cracks in the pavement
are pages in your diary,
detailing the days
of wasted waiting.

The day rivers rebelled,
your head full of warmer climes,
despite the iced hair
licking your face.

The face charming all.
You did not throw bricks,
granting the entrance
to the Malley's home.

Moving to the big city,
they took your best friend.
Promises to write
and insincere hopes.

The wish against fact.
Futile hopes never dying.
The map says: 'you are here,'
it is lying.

Broken
By Helen Raven

Millie

For the third time in the space of fifteen minutes, I check my watch. Picking up the cup of tea in front of me, I cradle it in my hands. I look out the window and scan the street. It's been eight years, would I recognize her?

"I hope that's black with two sugars," says a voice behind me. I turn around and stare at my former best friend. Fortunately, she hasn't changed much. She's dressed casually in jeans and a black coat, tied at the waist. Her blonde hair is pulled back into neat ponytail, outlining her razor sharp cheeks. Her cool blue eyes don't give away any emotion as she slips into the booth and sits down opposite me. Her red lips disappear into a straight line. She keeps her bag close to her as she shifts uncomfortably. "Hello Millie," she says, her voice cold and distant.

"I didn't think you were gonna come."

"Curiosity always gets the better of me," she replies.

"You look well," I say, hoping to break the ice with a compliment – even if she doesn't deserve one after everything.

The corners of her mouth lift up into a small smile but her eyes remain emotionless. There's a long silence. She rolls her eyes and leans forward against the table. I wait for her to speak.

She doesn't. I take a deep breath. Enough with trying to be nice.

"I slept with Joe." I haven't, I just know she's more likely to walk away if she thinks I have.

A flash of hurt passes through her face. The first bit of emotion she has shown since arriving. She stares at me, her blue eyes penetrating through mine. "You're joking." She says finally.
Shaking my head, I lean forward against the table between us, resting my arms before me.

"Ask him yourself."

She shifts uncomfortably in her seat and starts fiddling with a chain around her neck. She shakes her head again as if she doesn't believe me still. "You're lying."

I say nothing, but just sit back and wait for her to accept it.

"I don't believe you," she says. "This is just your idea of revenge."

I stiffen at the mention of my brother and narrow my eyes at her. "This has nothing to do with Sam," I say. "I'm not leaving this time. I'm here to stay."

Tamsin laughs. It's dry and raspy, as if she's trying to force herself into thinking this is some kind of joke. "Do you really think he's gonna finish with me for you? He's not gonna leave me. He loves me." She glances down at my stomach. Her face twists into a sneer. "Not to mention you're carrying another man's child, what man would want to be involved with you?"

"He's already cheated on you. Would he really do that if he loved you?" Ignoring the echo of doubt in the back of my mind, I clear my throat and meet her eye. "But that's not the real reason why I wanted to see you."

She narrows her eyes at me but says nothing. She sits back in her chair and picks up her mug of coffee. She takes a sip but holds it in between her hands. Her eyes never leave mine.

“I promise I won’t tell anyone if you leave,” I say. “What you did to Sam, how you set out to destroy him to get to me, will vanish if you do.”

“Ooh, I’m getting a strong sense of déjà vu.”

“I don’t want to tell Joe. He’s a nice guy, he doesn’t need to know that his ex-girlfriend is a psycho.”

Still she says nothing. She’s just staring at me. I can’t even read the expression on her face. Emotionless. “Yet he still slept with you behind my back. Yeah, really nice.”

“I don’t regret it.”

“You backstabbing little…” she hisses angrily. She stops and takes a deep breath, calming herself down. “Why couldn’t you just leave me alone? Leave *us* alone! We were happy without you.”

“Happy?” I say, matching her cool tone. “Your relationship is built on a lie.”

Silence.

“You told me you were pregnant with Joe’s child in hope I’d finish with him,” I blurt out angrily, in hope to provoke a reaction. Her silence is beginning to unnerve me. “You were my best friend and you lied so you could…” I splutter, struggling to remain calm. “…so you could have my boyfriend to yourself. Who does that?”

“And you told my parents,” she shrugs, unaffected by the accusation. “Two can play at that game, Millie.”

I force myself to calm down. “You nearly destroyed Sam’s life,” I say, quietly.

She rolls her eyes but says nothing.

“Why would you lie about something like that?” I ask. “Sam never touched you, why did you lie about him raping you?”

“Collateral damage.”

I say nothing. What can you possibly say to that?

“I only agreed to drop it because you promised you’d leave and never come back.” Tamsin leans forward. “We made a deal,” she hisses. “And yet here you are.”

“You have no shame, do you?”

“Speaking of your darling brother, how is Sam nowadays?” she asks, lifting her chin. “I hear he’s quite the businessman. That could be quite a downfall for him if I brought back those accusations and it would be all your fault for coming back.”

“And you’re still nothing but a bitter and twisted woman,” I shake my head in disgust and slide out of the booth as if to leave. “I guess some things just never change, do they?” I pick my bag up and sling it over my shoulder, pulling my coat around me in protection. “And because I’m not like you, I do wish that one day you’ll be happy.”

And without looking back, I walk out, leaving her and her empty threats behind.

Tamsin

There she is. I can see her under the street lamp. Millie looks left and right before crossing the road. I sit back in my car, my hands firmly gripping the steering wheel in front of me. She's not having him. How else to revenge Joe for cheating on me than hurting the most precious person in his life?

Revving the car, I wait for her to step into the road. She does so and I put my foot down, speeding forward. The roar of the engine makes her turn around. She looks me right in the eye, her face a picture of horror; her brown eyes are widen, a mixture of fear and confusion. Her face drains of colour, as she realizes what's going to happen and she opens her mouth, I hear her yell out. She covers her stomach, protectively. She tries to run. Too late.

And I can't help but smile.

Amentia
By T.R.J Shelley

Caleb hated his job. It was boring, underpaid and he always left filthy. Not to mention how he ached. He was seventeen for crying out loud; a bad back was supposed to be an old man's problem. Half of the time he wondered what the point was. Not just the job but everything. College? He sucked at anything even remotely academic. From maths to history he just couldn't get his head round it. Family? *Ha!* His parents despised him. He was just another mouth to feed, and a way of claiming more benefit money that would most likely be spent on fags and booze. What prospects did he have? He wasn't gonna get the grades to get into uni, nor was he gifted in the arts. He'd end up just like his dad, addicted to crap and constantly struggling to pay the bills.

At least at work he made a difference. As a cleaner, you see the before and after; the hard work paying off. He supposed it was worth it; after all, it was the one place he actually felt at home. Not to mention he worked by himself. There was nobody to piss him off. No little brother or sister to take what he'd earned by being mummy and daddy's favourite.

No, he was lucky. Most people didn't get a chance like he had. A lot of the others from the estate would have killed to land a job, earn a bit of cash, save up and get the hell away – just find a flat somewhere in a city where their prospects weren't shit awful. But life ain't fair, certainly not when you think about it for more than five minutes.

Unexpectedly, the door behind him creaked open. "Caleb, how are you getting on?"

"I'm doing fine, Mrs Eckles, nearly finished, just gonna start dusting the record collection."

"Wonderful. If you could organize them alphabetically when you put them back I'll throw in a few Jaffa cakes with your wages."

Caleb laughed, "Course I can, no problem at all."

"Excellent." Mrs Eckles smiled then closed the door behind her as she left. A few seconds later he heard the soft thud of her going back down the stairs. For an old lady she was alright. Every time he'd turn up for work she'd ask him how he was, listen to him talk about his hopes and his worries, you know, actually treated him like a human being, not like some folk. You know the ones. They look at you with a major napoleon complex, like you're some piece of dog crap they'd just stepped in. *Ah, sod it,* he thought. *No point getting angry about it. Won't change people. Best just get on with work.*

The record collection was huge. There was everything, from classical symphonies by well-known composers like Beethoven, Mozart, and Vivaldi to the Beatles. Hell, there was even some Billy Connelly in there! Records lined the entirety of the top shelves in the upstairs study. There must have been what? Hundreds of them? Maybe even a thousand? Caleb had never seen anything like it. Dust coated them completely. *This is gonna take a while...* He'd already dusted, vacuumed and polished everything else. This was all he had to do before he could go home for tea. Though, if he was being honest, he'd prefer to stay and work rather than go back to that abusive hell hole.

Slowly, methodically, he began to take the records down one by one and wiped them clean. Outside cover first, then inside. Mrs Eckles had pretty bad asthma, so he knew that getting rid of all the dust was a necessity. *No point doing a job half hearted. If you do it, you do it right, or don't bother.* He'd learnt that from watching his dad: he was on job seekers, constantly getting shitty jobs, then getting fired after a week, mostly for sheer laziness. It was too hard for him apparently, to work and be part of a functioning society. Caleb would never let himself be like that. Ever.

Time passed by. Apart from the faint melodic jangle of wind chimes that echoed outside, the clock striking half six was the only sound he'd heard since he'd started. Caleb yawned. An hour had passed since he began and he'd barely even made a dent in the collection. He had however managed to make a small pile of clean records, but it was taking far longer than he expected. Grabbing the next record from the shelf, he was contemplating rushing through, just doing the bare minimum and getting it done quickly, 'til he noticed that the record didn't say who it was by. There was no artist name, album title, nor composer.

He flipped it over. The back was the same. No text, no pictures – nothing. Confused and slightly curious, Caleb opened it up. The record lay in the centre, covered by two thin layers of plastic that he guessed were there to prevent the vinyl getting scratched. Usually he'd never take the record out, but he had an urge to, a temptation that he just couldn't resist.

Tentatively, he gently pinched the plastic sleeve and pulled it back, then took the record in his hands and walked over to the dust laden record player. Luckily he'd seen people use it once before on a T.V. show so he had a vague idea of how it worked. He plugged it in, put the record in place and moved the needle to gently rest on the disks grooved surface.

Nothing, the disk was rotating, the stylus was on top – it should have been making noise, but there was none. A bit anticlimactic. He really wanted to hear what was on it, but that's the thing about life, there's always questions to be asked. Answers are much harder to come by.

Shrugging his shoulders, he turned and went back to work, leaving the record playing as he continued cleaning. A few minutes passed by normally, then, all of a sudden, a strange ominous feeling washed over him. He felt his gut wrench. It was all he could do to hold down his lunch. It wasn't a pain, not really. More like unease. Anxiety.

Weakness consumed him. He could barely move. His head started to pound. His heart fluttered with exhaustion and his pulse began to skyrocket higher and higher. The room began to spin; his vision blurring until he could look no longer and shut his eyes.

He tried to call for help, tried to scream for Mrs Eckles, but his voice was no longer his to command. A sound jumped out at him, a high pitched wail, it burned his ears – destroyed his sanity. Voices whispered, their malicious intent growing louder and louder. He begged them to stop, to go away, but that only spurred them on. He was not their leader, no; he was theirs to command. A mortal vessel for their ambitions and he, like it or not, would do as instructed.

Caleb wriggled around, flailing and distressed, but the voices grew louder, dominant. They wouldn't tolerate his disobedience. Words hissed at him, like venomous missiles aimed straight at his heart. *"FAILURE! IDIOT!"* they cried in anguish.

He argued back, to no avail, for a part of him knew they spoke the truth. In the seventeen years he had walked the earth he had accomplished nothing of worth and most likely never would. They were right. He was a failure… he was a disappointment. What was the point of his existence, when no one cared whether he lived or died?

"NO!" Came another voice, this one familiar, yet alien all the same. It roared in contest, drowning out all contenders with its ferocity. "You are no failure. You still have time. Ignore those who seek to put you down. Strive forward, and live life to the fullest you can. Anything is possible!"

Bright white light blinded him. Caleb raised his hands to shield his eyes. After a few fleeting moments the light waned and his vision slowly returned. The study's chandelier hung above him; silver twinkling against the beige ceiling. It took him a few seconds to realize that he was lying down. How he got there he couldn't tell. He felt much better though. His head was fine, his thoughts clear – even his back seemed stronger.

Caleb sat up. *The record, it had to be the record!* He jumped to his feet and bolted over to the record player. It was there, plugged in, just as it had been before but the record had disappeared. *What the hell?* He span round, eyes scanning the room for any sight of it, but try as he might, he couldn't find it.

The door creaked open once more. Mrs Eckles walked in visibly worried. "Caleb? Are you okay? I heard banging…"

"I… I'm fine. I just…"

"You look pale, are you sure you're alright?"

"Yeah, I'm okay."

"Alright then, well, it's getting late, you should be getting off. You can finish the records next week."

"Okay." he mumbled. She started to close the door again. *Was it all just a dream?* He had to know. "Wait! Mrs Eckles, I was just wondering… did you move any of the records?"

"I've been downstairs, why? Has one gone missing?"

"Yes, it was right there on the player."

"It was actually in the player?" she asked. Caleb nodded. "How strange, the thing hasn't worked in donkey's years. Oh well don't worry about it. I'm sure there are a dozen more like it in the pile." Caleb wasn't so sure. That record was one of a kind. And now it was gone.

But he wasn't. He had a life to lead. He wasn't going to listen to the voices any more. He wasn't their slave. No. He was going to make something of his life, and prove them wrong.

Untitled (4)
By Uta Feinstein

Thunder and Lightning
By Alexandrea Cook

It’s not a sound you forget, no matter how many years have passed. It’s the embodiment of fear. It tears you from your bed and no matter the hour, you are always awake, fuelled by adrenalin. I reach for the essentials; they are all prepared in a neat little bag to the left of the door. This, after all, is not the first time. My young one first I plan; my eldest can take care of himself. The decision is made for me as I see him coming out of his sister’s room, a little person tucked within his arms, a small hand clenched on his night shirt. He whispers in her ear, soothing her cries.

I wish I could stop this moment. Freeze it in time. I want to reach out, place my hands on his shoulders and praise him, my wonderful boy. I don’t, I can’t, there isn’t time, at least not right now. Instead I push him gently towards the stairs.

It couldn’t have been more than a minute yet I could already hear them falling, sounds scattered between the constant groaning that already filled the streets.

“Hurry, Will. Go!” I say as he looks back at me for reassurance. Sometimes I forget he’s just a boy. He jostles his sister to reposition her on his side while grabbing the frame on the counter at the bottom of the stairs with his free hand.

“No, no, leave it!” I hear myself say. He ignores me. I’m glad he does. He knows it will comfort me, as well as them.

Katherine is starting to cry again. Lifting her head from her brother’s shoulder she looks for me. Seeing me right behind them, she takes comfort once again in her haven, listening to the soft murmurs of her brother’s voice. A comfort I cannot hear over the noise.

We’re out of the house now and the noise reflects that, but we don’t take note. Again we cannot afford to. We all know the risks, even my youngest knows how important it is to get there swiftly without any fuss. It's not far, a matter of seconds is all it takes, yet the short journey seems to take longer than normal. This isn't a new thought. Every night the warning sirens bring us out here and every night the distance to the shelter seems just one step further.

I breathe a sigh of relief the moment I close the shelter door behind me. I turn, watching as Will settles Katherine on the small wooden bed next to Martha. We share the shelter with next door, the Wilks family. Martha has two children, both boys. The youngest has his head laid in his mother's lap, the elder fiddling with the radio in the furthest corner of the Anderson. At the moment all he is succeeding in getting is a static buzzing, but every now and then a few notes of music weave their way through, just to be lost again. Will goes over to help; he always was good at tuning the radio, another skill he got from his father.

Katherine sits up and looks at me with watery eyes, the frame now rests in her tiny hands. She hates the raids; she always goes into one of her states. I can't seem to comfort her when she's like this, not like he could anyway. Once again I feel his absence as I move to sit next to her, bringing her head onto my lap, mirroring Martha's position. Martha meets my eyes momentarily but I look away quickly, feeling ashamed. What right do I have to miss my husband when at least he's still alive to be missed?

A part of me used to enjoy these nights in the shelter. I can't help but think just how selfish it is of me, that while our capital city is being ripped apart I longed for the excuse to be sealed away in the metal box, just to talk to Martha.

We used to share in an illusion, a simple escape from reality. For the few hours we spent together huddled with our children in this shelter, we talked about our husbands. We talked about their last letters; when they would be back; how proud they'd be of the kids; how we'd greet them cooking their favourite foods. Even our secret plans to sneak a few extra rashers of bacon from Brenda's for the occasion. We had it all worked out, going as far as to say we'd spend a week's rations on the one meal, all illogical promises for our men to return to us safely. It was strange, I always had this picture of them walking back down the street, shoulder to shoulder, dressed up fine and smart, arms slung about one another. Rather stupid actually; they were in different Units, different locations, they weren't even close friends when they we're back here. In fact I'd hear no end about their water drainage directed onto our land. Not to mention Martha's George would be a bit sharp about our joining fence, course that's all solved now, no fence to complain about with the shelter and all that.

It was all shattered with a single telegram.

Everybody sitting at home with a loved one at war both longed and dreaded a telegram. You needed news, any scrap of news that told you the condition of your loved one. As soon as you receive it, hold it in your hands, you take a moment to open it. You can't help but long for a promotion, or maybe even an injury. If, and unfortunately more likely, your telegraph contained neither of the above, you were left with missing in action or even worse, killed in action.

I can see it now, visible slightly at the edge of her pocket. It's been there three weeks. I didn't need to ask that day, what was written on the slip of paper. The sore eyes and silent tongue did most of the explaining. The small glimpse of hope in my eyes must have asked my question for me, missing or…?

No longer did we chat about what we'd do when our husbands came home.

"Run, rabbit, run, rabbit, run, run, run." The deep voice broke though hazy static, the two boys gave a yelp of triumph to which Martha and I shared a smile. The music formed an imperfect barrier to the sound of the air raids, even if it did very little to block it out, it returned a mirage of normality to the dim shelter.

Everyone seemed to lighten with the music. Katherine sat up from my lap, clutching the frame to her chest, quietly singing along. The boys were laughing in the corner, Will teasingly shoving the younger lad in the shoulder before ruffling his hair. Martha was combing her fingers through her youngest's hair soothingly, but her attention was on the two boys in the corner.

"I'm glad Will's got him to talk, laugh in fact, he's not been doing well." Martha spoke to me, her attention still on the two lads. We'd long since forgotten to be worried about being overheard, we learned early on that the raid, on top of the radio more than clouded our whispers. "It's not normal, you know, for him not to talk, just like George he is, always filling the silence." She smiles brokenly. "Are you worried? He's sixteen now, if they lower the requirements…" She gestures to Will, who was currently performing an impression of something or other causing the younger lad to laugh, oblivious that he was the subject of our convocation. Unknowingly, or maybe not so, she'd just voiced one of my deepest fears.

"Yes, lord, yes I'm worried." I still see him as my little boy, but even I'm not oblivious to the young man he's become. After all, how many times a day does he remind me of his father? "But they won't lower it, and this war'll be over soon I'm sure, it has to end eventually."

Even to my ears it sounds optimistic, a far cry that is contradicted by the nearing sounds. It's almost too loud to talk now; it feels as if they are right above us. I can just make out the radio, 'In the mood' I think, in the background but it's eclipsed by the vibrations echoing around the shelter. They're getting closer, closer than they've been before.

It's a lot like thunder and lightning. You hear the hoarse sound, a mix between a whisper and a whistle. Seconds later you hear the explosion, sometimes its distant, other times the vibrations run through you. It's a lot like thunder and lightning except it isn't. And you just wish it was.

The boys have stopped messing around, turning for silence instead. I stare at Will across the shelter, clutching Katherine tighter to me as she cries into my night dress. I cover her ears with my hands. He must have sensed my fear, as he came over quickly, sitting beside me, leaning against my side, his head on my shoulder. I rest my chin on top of his head, trying and failing not to jump at every bomb. I see him reach out and place his hand on top of his sisters which is clenching the frame. For a moment I feel like we're all together again, my children protected by the love of both their parents. It is a foolish feeling, what protects them is this cold hard metal shell, but it's a nicer thought than the truth.

We all cry out as the ground shakes.

"Dear God, what was that?" Martha asks, looking worriedly at me. It was a building collapsing, she'd guessed that as much as I.

At this moment I didn't care. I see that like me, she holds both her children. All that matters is the children in my arms, and they are both well.

It's silent now, but though our grips have loosened we stay in the same position. The silence is almost as frightening as the bombs, dare you hope…

The all clear siren sounds. Still it takes us a moment to gather the nerve to leave the shelter, apprehensive to step outside.

The smell is the first thing that hits me.

It's the faint, sickly, chemical scent of burning plastic which is almost overwhelmed by the smell of burning wood. I feel the smoke cling to my throat. Katherine, who stands to my right holding my hand, coughs lightly at the change in air quality. We are quickly joined by the rest of the shelter. Will hands me the frame as he steps out, Katherine must have let go of it in all the noise. He doesn't say anything. Nobody does. At least not for a moment. Instead we look past our fences to a few houses down. Two to be exact, Martha's house, her far side neighbour and then… smoke, just lots of smoke. I can hear yells and sirens, of a different type, coming closer. I look at our houses, standing strong side by side unaffected, then I look at the absence, that once stood an identical structure. Will's coughing now, and I have to resist the sharp tickling in my lungs.

"We should get them inside, can't be good for them to breathe this in. Us neither I suppose." Martha's small coughs cause her words to stutter, but I still hear them.

"You're right, I'll see them inside before going over to see-"

"See the damage to the building. They should be ok, they were sharing Lucy's shelter, they'll be ok." Her voice is strong, but her eyes show her worry, mirroring my own. I just nod, pushing my two back towards the house. Will takes Katherine's hand from mine, leading them both inside. I grab my bag from the shelter before following them.

By the time I get inside, they're already halfway up the stairs. Will is holding Katherine the same way his father used to, she's already falling asleep on his shoulder.

"I'll be up in a minute, Will, get yourself to bed," I whisper, not wanting to wake her up. He just smiles tiredly and continued going up the stairs, making shushing sounds as the jolting starts to wake her.

I'm standing in front of the counter at the bottom of the stairs. The frame in my hands. I know that the picture in this frame should be the one in his uniform, the picture he got taken the day he left. The one showing him fulfilling his duty for his country. It's not. It's the picture we had taken three weeks before then, when we all pitched in digging for the shelter. He's got a shovel in one hand his arm slung over Will's shoulder, Katherine rested on his side, waving to the camera. He's dressed in a torn, muddy shirt; in fact all three of them are covered in dirt. I prefer this one. It's the one showing him fulfilling his duty for his family. I place it back on the counter.

When I go to check on them, my youngest first, I find her tucked in my eldest's arms. He opens his eyes as he hears me enter, and I set myself on the side of the bed next to my children.

"Come to rescue me?" He gestures to the two little hands still tightly glued to his night shirt. I smirk at his predicament.

"Nope, this is payback years in the making, you were worse than she is." He groans jokingly in response and tries to gently pry her away with little success. He finally gives up. I push him back gently so he is lying down, before covering them both with a blanket.

"Thank you for looking after her, Will," I whisper, moving my son's hair out of his eyes.

'Don't really have a choice, do I?' he gestures again to the vices on his shirt. His eyes are shut now; arms wrapped round his little sister. I tuck them both in tighter.

"Yes you do, my wonderful boy."

Marshes Hill
By Cara Da Silva

Pounding squidgy heart, chasing country lanes,
Two stroke petrol steering, gripping, zooming to a halt,
Hair tangled, leather plonking pebbles.
Upon a dark peachy night, Marshes Hill awoke.
Silence… drifting mid-air, washing thoughts away,
Eyes awestruck, perceiving glory,
Luxury magical surprise
My love, a whimsical impulse,
Ascending, adventurous grass.
Carefree embrace, light as a red fairy,
Gazing his succulent soft lips,
Tightly closing, innocent endeavour.
A paradigm of beauty,
Arousing lynx essence, fluffy mind urging,
Wanted, together, ecstasy,
Lifting Marshes Hill with us.

Bird-Brained
By Oliver Gillespie

I once had a cousin who had a thing for heights; though not in the way you might expect. He would always climb to the highest floor, the highest step, the highest rung of a ladder. He would conquer these summits and claim them as his own.

We would usually leave him to it, let him be. That is, until we saw the look in his eye: that suspicious glint of clear, warning blue. He would look down on us below, then give a wild shout and throw himself majestically into the air. His eyes would swell in triumph, his arms would spread wide and then, in a graceful arc, he would accelerate straight into the floor.

We couldn't stop him. When we lived in a flat, he threw himself off the balcony. He would yell in ecstasy as he fell through the air, only to plummet into the pavement and startle the pedestrians below. Sometimes he would flap his arms, but it never helped him. He broke all sorts of bones; we were forever taking him to the hospital. He was a danger to himself. In the end, my father had to fit bars across the windows to prevent his deluded flights of fantasy.

Whenever I asked why, he met my eyes and gave a wry smile.

“I was born to fly,” he said. “'My mother did it, my father did it. If they could do it, then why can't I?”

Ode to Late Night BBC Three
By Matthew Lewis Miller

Following half hour trajectories,
in methodical arcs, they wipe away
the evening, leaving tiny islands of rain
that never build into floods, not a smear
on the bright transparent. Like the remains
of an insect (that must have seen this enough
to know what happens next), my head wails soft
tinnitus, as I'm chopped up by wipers, and sucked
into the engine. I drag my massacred corpse to bed,
to reincarnate and come back for tomorrow's collision.

The Director
By T.R.J. Shelley

The director knows what he wants.
A wife, big house, money and success.

But the boy,
the boy is lost…

Lost adrift in a dream all his own,
stuck replaying memories of monkey bars, sandcastles and tag,

while the director struggles
with the mundane, monotonous stress of life…

But the boy,
the boy is free…

Free to run, to laugh and play,
to daydream half his life away.

The director,
he works in his office,
boring and mild.

But the boy,
he's off on an African safari.
Untamed. Wild.

The director looks up.
Stares straight at the baby blue sky,

But when the boy tries to do the same,
he can't.
It's black.
His whole life is a lie…

For the director its summer,
warm and light.
But the boy hears only thunder,
death's delight.

As the director looks out the window one final time,
he closes his eyes,
and sees the boy,
to his mind's surprise.

The boy looks up at him,
his face contorted in a primal,
animalistic,
hate filled scowl,

and simply says…

"What happened to me?"

A Letter to Myself, Aged 13 ½
By Amy Maidment

You have a long way to go.

You look up at the cliffs,
Dreaming of what's on the other side
And of the secrets they hide,
But you do nothing.
You just look up and feel small.

You have a long way to go.

You are not alone, but you feel it.
You think a boyfriend's the thing to have,
A necessity you lack,
But you don't understand.
Love is not owned, it is stumbled upon.

You have a long way to go.

You shy away from your friends,
But your timidness is a learned reaction,
A safety contraption;
You are a universe of madcap ideas.
If they laugh, it just means they don't understand.

You have a long way to go.

If Words Could Talk
By Sara Assumani

If words could talk, they would say that my heart
has surpassed an eclipse.
I was obscured by my own insecurity and
inability to function without you, so much so
that I thought maybe if you left I would break in two
and again into four,
until the pieces of me became as extinct as
the beating hearts of the dead.
My infinite obligation to love you
is in fact not an obligation at all.
It is a desire,
and an inclination for your paternal approval.
Your rock-sturdy disposition
is the foundation that keeps me tall at 5ft2,
I love you *papa* and perhaps before
you never knew
just how much you mean to me.
But now you know there is nothing stronger
than my fierce ability to protect you
as you have protected me,

Every day of my life.

Reflection of a Festival
By Kaya Gromocki

Taken at Shambala Festival, Northamptonshire

How to Care For Your Pet Poet
By Kimberly Jamison

So you've decided to get a poet
Or Poetam to use the scientific term.
This is a creature to be treated with kindness
But remember you have got to be firm.

If yours is the long haired variety
(And many are)
Prepare for moulting season.
Hair everywhere. Kitchen, bathroom, car.
You've got to feed your sensitive soul
With tails of revolutionaries
Protests and issues
But nothing too scary.
They like ornaments around them
Maybe a treasure chest, or scuba diver
Lots of blankets and cushions
Or even a broken typewriter.
Prepare for constant ink stained hands
And pleas for a cup of tea
And remember to let them in the house at night
Because they'll probably have lost their key.
Their days are longer
Because they're all insomniacs
Or hypochondriacs
And no they can't spell that.

Every now and again
But don't be too harsh
They need a 40ml dose of reality
And a good kick up the arse.

Satisfaction
By Matthew Lewis Miller

I have an itch.

It begins in the backs of my knees and spreads
through my legs to the top of my head
and the tips of my fingers.

Sometimes it is
not noticeable.
I can take my mind off it, but
whenever I am not
scratching,
it is there.
Somewhere.
Dormant but ready to flare.

Scratching this itch
feels good,
most of the time.

But –

I'm scared to scratch my itch.
What if I become addicted to the sensation
and cannot ever stop?
When will I sleep, or go to the shops?

What if I itch so hard and for so long
that my soft skin breaks and I begin
to bleed and enjoy
the feeling of that blood on my fingertips
and so keep peeling until any disease
can peer in at my flesh and pick it apart?

What if I enflame the offending area and build
ugly blisters all over my body that

disfigure my face and mark me out
in bus-stops as untrustworthy?
What if I fall through my own pores
so entirely that
I lose the sight of the sun, or sofas,
or nights in? or out? or anywhere
but my own head?

What if it never leaves?

What if madness?

After a quick itch,
all of these questions
fade
and I'm left feeling
deliciously new,
like a tight-fit, shop-bought t-shirt,
left surrounded by growing mountains
of paper
and one small
re-built molehill
of satisfaction.

I have an itch.

It begins

Diamonds
By Liam Powell

We've got this sorted. I know the score, done it a million times before. Get in, get out, and get the fuck out of there as soon as possible. The Bill will be on us in minutes. No time to hang around, we're there for one reason. Diamonds.

When you're breaking into a jeweller's you need a plan. Go in there without one and see what happens. Enjoy your prison showers, fella, let's see if someone takes a liking to you. Before anything else, you need a leader. If you don't have one, get one. If you don't get one, don't do the fucking job. We've got a leader: Arnie. That's not his real name; like he's going to hand that out. Never know when you've got a snake in the grass. The Bill catches someone, make sure they've got nothing to say about anyone else. Lesson one. You want to say your name, you may as well tell the bloke which prison you'd like. Give bullshit names, whatever you like, just not your actual fucking name.

So, we've got Arnie in charge. Knows what he's doing, his plan sounds good. Do things as he says, we should be alright. Should be. Don't take anything for granted in this game. But he's talking sense, clearly knows the place we're hitting – where the cameras are, where the guards are, where the stones are. I don't get impressed. But if I got impressed, then I would be impressed.

Jimmy and Freddy go in first, carrying the biggest shotguns you'll ever see. Scare the crap out of everyone and if not, fucking blow the crap out of everyone. They can take their pick, so long as they shut up. They go straight to the counter, make sure that bastard doesn't press the alarm. Following Jimmy and Freddy are me, Deano, Steve and Roger. Two go left, two go right, get them customers in the corners. The workers can join them if they like, or they can be a hero. Want to be a hero? You've got balls, but not for much longer.

Everyone's quiet, that's vital. We've got Eric keeping look out, but the less nosy fuckers outside the better. Jimmy and Freddy take care of the stones – the bloke behind the counter will hand them over, don't worry about that. Sixteen million worth. Those shiny little fuckers will make us rich. What'd I say? Arnie knows his stuff. This is a proper joint.

Once we've got the stones we get out. Sharpish. Everyone into a couple of cars, and we're gone. Enjoy the rest of your day, ladies and gents. We're not stupid. There's drivers, and they're not getting shit. They drive us back to Arnie's hideout, get a few grand each, and fuck off.

Once in the hideout, we work out if we've been followed. Any of the Bill around, waiting to crash the place the second those stones jump on the table? Give that job a few minutes, if everyone's done their jobs properly we should be fine. Should be. Arnie's bloke turns up half an hour after us. Some Indian bloke, couldn't care less what his name is. As long as he hands over sixteen big ones. Split that eight ways, and it's Cheerio, fellas. Get on with your lives, buy what the fuck you want, and let's never meet again.

That's all that's been running through my head this morning – two big ones in my back pocket at the end of this job. If we get caught, I reckon we're looking at ten years each. Arnie probably more. The leader always get a couple extra, just for good measure. Be a good little boy, and you'll be out in seven, maybe seven and a half. Fuck that. Nearly eight years inside, I'd rather the two million.

We get to the hideout, me and Roger. We come in pairs, leaving ten minutes in between each pair. Me and Roger are second – fine by me. Fuck being first, fuck being last. Roger's about thirty, has a scar on his neck and has brown hair, that's all I know about him. That's all I want to ever know. Oh, and his name isn't Roger.

The hideout's a warehouse, an empty one in middle of fuck knows where. Some place, twenty minutes from the shop.

Everyone's in suits, me included. That's Arnie's orders. Usually suits stand out, but the place we're hitting no suits stand out. Lesson two. Don't stand out. Not until you're in the place anyway. The hideout is fine by me, I've done jobs before, and this is a better hideout than most.

Arnie does the talking, runs everyone through what they're doing. Nobody else says shit. This has been planned a few weeks now, so anyone who doesn't know what they're doing, run off home to your playhouse, you stupid fuck. Everyone knows though. Arnie's in charge and he wants it right, so we go through it again. No alarms, everyone in the corners, grab the stones under the desk, make sure there's ten little bags of them, get the fuck out. Sounds simple. It isn't.

You get pussies. Everyone's a loudmouth when the planning's going on, act the big man with a gun pointing in some random fucker's face. But the day comes and they freeze. Lesson three. Don't freeze. You freeze, you're fucked. These guys look the business, but who knows what's happening in seven other heads. It's a nervous atmosphere, just before you do a job. Everyone's excited, but at the same time everyone's shitting themselves. We haven't got away with it until everyone splits with their shares, and even then you have to watch your back.

Arnie's finished talking, everyone looks happy enough with the plan. That's a good start, now go out there and execute the fucking plan. Everyone's up and sorting things out, making sure the guns are secure and things like that. There's a bit of noise, nothing too heavy though – everyone's focussed. These two blokes have shown up, the drivers I take it. Ok, don't just stand there. I don't give a shit what you look like, just drive the fucking car and make sure the Bill don't catch us.

Everyone's walking outside, the cars are waiting. Split up, four plus a driver to one, three plus a driver to another. We've already sorted who's with who, I'm with Deano,

Steve and Roger – the four who control the customers. The engines are revving, we can see the world acting as though it's a normal day. This isn't a normal day, this is the day I take two fucking million. The first car's gone, now it's us. The driver pulls in front of some shitty red Jeep, and shoots off after the other car. Alright, let's go.

Smokey Fir
By Kaya Gromocki

Taken in Alderly Edge, Cheshire

Traveller
By Keira Andrews

Twin
brothers.
Wing span – stretched,
swooping, diving;
circles in the air.
Mimicking white rapids
underneath the water's dance.
The weather-beaten rocks cry out
as the pounding froth entombs below.
In the pale winter's sun, the snow's drift falls.

The rushed reflection sparkles with black smoke,
as the steam train rhythmically beats through
the concaved hills, where newborn lambs
take first steps in grassy fields.
Ancient stone bridges arch
over ruptured tracks,
as travellers
pass under
two lone
hawks.

The Red Scarf
By Helen Raven

The woman at the next table was reading. Her head was down, eyes glued to the page. Laura Brydon watched her intensely. She took in the woman's dark hair tumbling down her back, the pale skin, the jagged scar along her jawline. She was dressed casually in a vintage black dress with a red bow on the front, and a gold shawl hung from the back of the chair behind her. Laura usually didn't suffer from nerves nor was she shy, but she was having trouble trying to find the courage to approach this woman, a woman who she believed to be her mother. They had the same dark hair, the same pale skin and clearly both shared a love for vintage clothing, but there was something else about this woman that made Laura doubt herself. She had only ever had one photograph of her mother, and in that picture, she didn't have a scar. No, she looked happy, she looked young and vibrant. Grinning at the camera, her arms were thrown around a guy around the same age, a young man Laura knew to be her father.

In the picture, the woman was wearing a red scarf, beautifully woven and designed, the very scarf that Laura was holding in her hand. The only thing her father had that belonged to her mother. Laura took out the faded photograph from her school blazer pocket and unfolded it. She placed it on the table in front of her, and smoothed it out. She was aware of how creased it looked from the amount of times she had folded ~~it~~ and unfolded it over the years, but she treasured it, carried it everywhere with her. Her mother was beautiful – is beautiful. She glanced over at the woman sitting at the next table. It was definitely her. It had to be.

Taking a deep breath, Laura picked up the photo, folded it in half and put it back in her pocket along with the red scarf. She didn't want spook the woman. She stood up and headed towards the woman's table.

The woman must have heard her because she looked up. Her eyes fell on Laura, standing in front of her. Blue eyes, Laura noted. Laura, herself, had inherited her father's chestnut brown. The woman folded the corner of her page, marking her place and closed her book. Up close, the scar looked aggressive, jagged and red raw but the woman still looked beautiful, there was no doubt about that. Laura tried not to stare at the scar. The woman reached for her shawl behind her and draped it over her shoulders as if ready to make a quick dash if needs be. "Can I help you?"

"Are you Eva John?" Laura found the words tumbling out of her mouth before she could stop herself. She hadn't planned on being so blunt and abrupt.

The woman frowned. "I don't go by that name anymore," she replied.

Laura took a deep breath, forcing herself to calm down. "My name is Laura Brydon," she said.

A flash of recognition passed through the blue eyes at the name of 'Brydon' but Eva said nothing. If anything, she looked startled.

"My father is Richard Brydon," she said. "I believe you knew him about sixteen years ago," she added.

"You'd better sit down," Eva whispered.

Laura did as she was told. She felt slightly dazed. She was finally sitting face to face with her mother. She had been dreaming about this for as long as she could remember. Time and time again, she'd pictured herself having that one conversation with her mother, wanting to know why she left, why she walked out on them. But right now, she didn't know how she felt. Did she feel angry, or sad? She had never expected it to be a happy reunion. She wasn't sure if she felt any sort of emotion right now. The whole thing suddenly made her feel overwhelmed. She just sat still.

"Does your father know you're here?" asked Eva, in a quiet voice.

"No," answered Laura. "Are you married?" she asked. 'Is that why you don't go by the name of John anymore?"

"I'm divorced," said Eva. "But I kept my married name for professional reasons."

"What do you do?"

"I'm a photographer," she said. "My husband, ex-husband…" she corrected herself. "…And I own a modelling agency, we run the business together."

"Sounds impressive."

"Look," Eva leant forward on the table and Laura found herself drawn into those cool blue eyes. "What has Rich, I mean, your father told you about me?"

Laura shrugged, the nerves were beginning to ease away. Maybe this wasn't going to be so bad after all. "He doesn't talk about you," she said honestly. "He gets angry and shuts himself off into his study when I mention you."

Eva nodded. "Understandable," she says quietly. "I hurt him pretty bad."

"What happened?" asked Laura. She had always been curious as to why her dad had always refused to talk about her mum. Why he only had a red scarf and no pictures of her on display. It only made her think the worst. And her imagination was known to run wild.

Eva was quiet for a moment, her blues eyes looking Laura up and down. “You see this?” Eva lifted a finger and traced her scar across her jaw up to her left ear. Laura couldn’t help but notice the manicured nail. Her own nails were short; she chewed them all the time.

Laura nodded. How could she miss it?

“This is the reason why I left, Laura,” said Eva, using her name for the first time.

Laura frowned. “I don’t understand,” she said, shaking her head. Then her eyes widened. “Did dad do that to you?”

Eva shook her head. “Of course not,” she said quickly, lying her hand on Laura’s on the table. “Your father never hurt me; he never laid a finger on me.” Laura looked down at their hands on the table, the gesture felt so comfortable and so right. Eva saw her watching, and withdrew her hand before clearing her throat, misinterpreting Laura’s gaze. “How did you find me?”

“I did some research.” Laura pulled out the red scarf out of her pocket. “I think this belongs to you.” She put it down on the table in front of them. Eva stared at it. She put her hands to her mouth, stifling her gasp. She picked it up, not quite believing that it was real.

She let out a little laugh. “I can’t believe he kept this,” she whispered.

“What happened?” asked Laura again. “Why won’t dad talk of you? Why did you walk out on him, on us?”

Eva looked down at the table. She was still playing with the scarf, wrapping it around her hands, feeling the material between her fingers. “I was in a car accident a few days after you were born," she said. "Thankfully you weren't in the car with me. You were with your dad."

"Is that how you got the scar?" asked Laura.

Eva nodded. She looked up, and their eyes met. "And other injuries. I suffered from retrograde amnesia." She closed her eyes and shook her head, a painful expression passing over her face. There was a beat of silence, her eyes opened, this time shining with tears. "It meant that when I came around, I couldn't remember certain things…"

Laura sat back in her chair as she realized what Eva was saying, the penny finally dropped. "Like the fact that you had a daughter."

"Exactly."

"But you remember now?" asked Laura. "I mean, you know who I am, right?"

"Gradually over the years, my memory came back," said Eva. "I started having visions, or dreams, if you like, of giving birth and holding a baby in my arms, and Richard was there too. I asked my mother about it, she confirmed that it was true."

"Then why didn't you come back? Why didn't you try and find me?"

"I had met my husband by then," whispered Eva, chewing down on her lip. "And I tried to contact Richard but my mum told me that he didn't want to see me again."

Laura frowned. "I don't understand," she said. "Surely he knew you'd get better, surely he'd stick around to help with your memory."

Laura watched as Eva swallowed. She fiddled with her hair, and shifted uncomfortably in her chair. "Laura, I want you to understand that me and your dad were both very young back then," she said, this time taking Laura's hand and holding onto it. "I'd just turned 18 and…'

"And what?"

"I was in a car with another man," said Eva, quickly. She took a deep breath. "Sadly he died at the scene," she added, and Laura let go of her mother's hand. "He was a friend, a close friend, but Richard didn't stick around either way. I guess the fact that I couldn't remember him didn't exactly help matters."

"That would explain a lot," said Laura.

"But he kept this," whispered Eva, speaking to herself more than Laura. She was looking down at the red scarf. She lifted it to her face and held it there as if breathing in the scent. Tears slid down her cheeks as she closed her eyes again.

"Did you ever think of me?" asked Laura. "You know, when you remembered?"

Eva opened her eyes. She lowered the scarf and for the first time, her painted red lips twisted into a smile. "Of course," she said. "It's one of the reasons why my husband and I finally split up." She shook her head. "I have regular visits from Richard's mother, though."

"You're in contact with Grandma Brydon?"

"Yes," said Eva. She reached over for her handbag and fumbled inside for something. She drew out a photograph and passed it to Laura. "We meet twice a year, have done ever since my memory came back. She didn't agree with Richard's view on not allowing me in your life so she brought me photos of you as you grew up. That's my favourite one, the one I carry around everywhere, the one I show off."

Laura looked down at the picture in front of her and felt herself instantly smile. It was one of her favourites too; she had it framed on her bedroom wall. It was a picture of herself and her father on their last holiday in the Alps last summer for her 16th birthday. They were standing side by side, her dad's arm around her, both of them grinning at the camera. They had asked a passer-by to take the picture for them.

"Laura!" Both of them jumped at the sound of Laura's name being shouted across the street. A few other people looked around at the angry voice. Laura heard herself groan as she spotted her dad storming toward them. She glanced at Eva. The woman's eyes had widened and, if it was possible with someone with naturally pale skin, had paled enormously. She rose from her chair as Richard Brydon approached, looking furious.

"Dad," Laura jumped up from her own seat and greeted him as he came to abrupt stop in front of their table. His eyes focused on Eva and for a moment, his face blanched at the sight of her. There was not a flicker of warmth or even a smile. His face arranged itself into the look he always wore just before he exploded with anger.

"Laura," he said quietly, his voice cool but dangerous. His eyes never left Eva's. "Go home."

"Hello Richard," said Eva. A ghost of a smirk flickered across her face.

He was practically shaking with anger. "You poisonous little witch."

"Dad!" Laura couldn't keep the shock out of her voice.

“Every word she’s said to you is a lie, Laura, she’s poison,” said her dad, his eyes still on Eva. Her eyes wide, Laura looked at Eva for some sort of denial, but the woman’s face remained passive.

“But the scar on your face?” questioned Laura finally when no one spoke. Her eyes darted back to the vicious red line that crossed Eva’s jawline.

Her dad’s eyes still never left Eva’s face. “Ahh, you used the car crash story, didn’t you?”

Eva said nothing and cocked her head to the side, ever so slightly and signalled for dad to carry on. An amused expression twisted itself onto her face.

“She did it herself. She fell down on some glass in the street when she was drunk out of her face,” said dad, shooting Eva a look so cold it made Laura shiver. “The picture in your hand,” he added. “Look on the back.”

Laura did as she was told. She turned it over. On the back was her dad’s familiar scrawl. *Over the years you’ve sent back all the letters and photos of your daughter, this is the last. Your daughter is beautiful and you’ve missed out on watching her grow up. I hope all your lies and twisted bitterness was worth it.*

Laura felt her heart sink, and stomach drop. It was lies. Everything that Eva had told her. And she’d been a fool to believe it. She looked up at Eva, hoping for an explanation. But none came.

Instead, Eva narrowed her eyes, focused on Richard and completely blanking Laura. “All these years and you still hold a grudge,” she said, her voice dripping with ice. “It’s pathetic, really.”

"If you walk away now," Richard said, struggling to remain calm. "Then we'll pretend this never happened."

And to Laura's horror, that's exactly what Eva did. Placing the red scarf on the table, she walked away and never looked back.